THE ENOR

THE
ENORMOUS EGG

by Oliver Butterworth

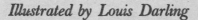

Illustrated by Louis Darling

A YEARLING BOOK

To Michael, Timothy, Dan and Kate
who are my closest critics

Published by
Dell Publishing
a division of
Bantam Doubleday Dell Publishing Group, Inc.
666 Fifth Avenue
New York, New York 10103

Louis Darling, who drew the pictures for this book, would like to express his thanks to Dr. Edwin H. Colbert and Mrs. Rachel Nichols of the American Museum of Natural History. They supplied models of Triceratops and Protoceratops, after whom the young animal was drawn, answered many questions and were helpful in every way possible.

The trademark Yearling® is registered in the U.S. Patent and Trademark Office.

The trademark Dell® is registered in the U.S. Patent and Trademark Office.

ISBN: 0-440-72337-X

Reprinted by arrangement with Little, Brown and Company (Inc.), in association with The Atlantic Monthly Press.

Printed in the United States of America

November 1986

10 9 8 7 6 5

RAD

Chapter One

MY NAME IS NATE TWITCHELL, BUT I CAN'T help that. It's a kind of a funny name, but I've had it for twelve years, and I'm pretty much used to it by now. And I guess a lot of other folks have got used to it too, after the thing that happened up here in Freedom last summer. That's the name of the town I live in — Freedom, New Hampshire. It's just a little town, with a few houses all along one street, and a store and a church, and not much else. Oh yes, and a school. I almost forgot that. We're only about three miles from the Maine state line, but Pop says Freedom's just as much a part of our state as Concord is, and *somebody* has to live near the State of Maine.

My pop runs a newspaper here in town. It's called the *Freedom Sentinel*, and it comes out once a week. We mail out a lot of copies to people in Effingham and Center Ossipee and places like that. I guess the paper doesn't make much money, but we have some chickens and a goat and a vegetable garden, and that helps out.

But I want to tell you about this thing that happened to us. I don't know just where to begin. I guess I better go back to last spring, when Mrs. Parsons began leaving her window open. You see, she sleeps with her bedroom window shut all winter, but when it warms up again in May, she begins leaving her window open at night. Pop always waits for Mrs. Parsons to open that window before he plants his beans. He says it's more dependable than the almanac.

Anyway, her house is next to ours, and her window looks out on our back yard where the chicken coop is, and last spring she began to complain to Mom that the rooster was waking her up with his crowing. She said we ought to get rid of him.

We had a family conference the next morning at breakfast. Mom said we didn't have any right to disturb the neighbors, just because we wanted to keep an old rooster. Pop said he thought we might have the *right* to disturb the neighbors, but we'd better not disturb Mrs. Parsons because she lets us keep our goat in her back lot. Cynthia (she's my sister) said she didn't care what happened to the nasty old bird. That made me kind of mad, because we've had that old rooster for six years now, and I like him. My Uncle Julius brought him over to us from his farm in Potter Place. He's a New Hampshire

Red — the rooster, I mean — and he's got a wild look in his eye and always runs at my sister with his wings flapping whenever he gets a chance. She hates him.

Anyway, I said we ought to try some way of keeping the rooster quiet in the early morning, and if it worked, then we could keep him, and Mrs. Parsons could get her sleep, and everything would be all right.

"And how do you propose to keep a rooster quiet?" Pop wanted to know. "Crowing at daybreak is a pretty strong habit with roosters."

"Couldn't we shut him up somewhere at night?" I said. "We could put him down cellar, and it would be dark and he wouldn't know when it was time to crow."

Mom never really enjoys having any of the livestock in the house, and she didn't take to the idea, even when I promised to clean out his box every morning, but Pop said why don't

we try it for a while and see how it works. "After all," he said, "we don't want to sentence him without a trial. If we did that sort of thing up here in Freedom, it would be a bad example to the rest of the country."

In the end Mom agreed to give it a try, and I was going to have the job of taking Ezekiel down cellar every night and letting him out in the morning. We called the rooster Ezekiel after a great-uncle of mine. Pop says it's important to keep a name like that in the family.

Well, for about a month I went on carrying Ezekiel down into the cellar every night and carrying him out again in the morning. He didn't like it a bit, and used to put up an awful fuss in the evening when I tried to catch him. When I picked him up off the roost he would squawk and beat his wings in my face, and feathers and dust would blow all around and the hens would get all roused up and everything. I got kind of tired doing it every day, and sometimes I wondered if it was worth while doing all that just for a rooster. But you know how it is when you're doing something that's your own idea. You just can't back down and let people say I told you so. So I kept at it, and there got to be a lot of feathers scattered around the cellar. Sometimes about three o'clock in the morning you could hear old Ezekiel whooping it up down there, but it was pretty muffled, and the rest of the family didn't say anything about it.

It was just about the middle of June when this peculiar thing happened. For about a week I had noticed that one of the hens was looking pretty queer. She had swelled out quite a bit, and was lopsided, and her feathers stuck out all over, the way a hen gets when she's too worried to smooth herself down. Pop thought she was just broody and wanted to set, and he told me to keep shooing her off the nest, but I had an idea it was something more than that. She got so big she could hardly waddle, and I didn't have the heart to push her off the nest once she climbed up to it. So all that week she just sat there getting more and more bulgy, and looking more and more surprised at herself. Then one morning when I carried Ezekiel out to the chicken yard I looked in the henhouse to see how this hen was getting along, and my gosh, there was the biggest egg I'd ever seen. It was so big it took up just about the whole nest, and there was the hen teetering on the edge of the box with her head tilted to one side, looking at that egg as if she couldn't figure out what it was. I touched it, and it had a kind of leathery shell, more like a turtle egg, and it was a sort of longish shape and big as a mushmelon, or even bigger maybe.

I ran back to the house and yelled out that our hen had just laid the biggest egg in the world, and hurry up and look at it before it explodes or something. We all tore out to the henhouse, and I was afraid the egg would be gone, but there it was, and the hen was sitting on top of it, doing her best to cover it. She looked kind of puzzled, as if this wasn't quite what she had expected, but she was going to make the best of it anyway. I sort of admired her for that.

Pop thought it was some kind of a trick at first, and he looked at me out of the corner of his eye. But when we lifted the hen off the egg and looked it over carefuly, they all agreed it was a real egg, but a queer one. Pop scratched his head and looked at the chicken, and then at the egg, and then back to the chicken again. "It doesn't seem possible," he said. "The egg's almost as big as she is. How could she do it?"

"But what will we do with it?" my sister asked.

"We could all have it for breakfast," Pop suggested. "How many minutes would you boil an egg that size?"

"We will *not* have it for any breakfast," Mom said. "I won't have that thing in my kitchen. It looks like a snake's egg to me."

"Some snake," Pop said.

But I asked why not keep it and let the hen sit on it till it hatched, and then we could see what would come out of it.

"Nothing good, I'm certain of that," Mom said. "It would probably be something horrible. But just remember, if it's a crocodile or a dragon or something like that, I won't have it in my house for one minute."

"Very well, Mrs. Twitchell," Pop said, winking at me. "We'll promise not to bring any dragons into the house." He lifted the hen back on top of the enormous egg, and she slipped around and fluttered her wings trying to get her balance up there. We all went back to the house for breakfast. Pop said that egg would give him something besides local gossip to put in the newspaper for a change.

Cynthia wasn't as excited about the big egg as I was, but she would have been if she'd known what was going to hatch out of it.

Chapter Two

TAKING CARE OF THAT EGG WAS AN AWFUL chore. The trouble was that the thing was so big that the poor hen couldn't handle it. You see, when a hen sits on her eggs, she keeps turning them over every now and then so they'll get warmed evenly all around. I guess everyone must know that anyway, but Pop says when you're writing something you can't take *anything* for granted, because you never know who might read it. So if I start explaining something you know about already, just skip that part and go on. I suppose there might be somebody who'd lived in a city all his life, and he wouldn't know too much about how a hen takes care of her eggs and things like that. So I guess I better take Pop's advice and explain things as I go along. He must know what he's talking about, what with his newspaper and all.

Well, this hen couldn't budge that big egg, so I had to come in three or four times a day and turn it over for her. I piled the straw up good around it to help keep it warm, and between the two of us we managed pretty well in the daytime, but it kept me kind of busy. Luckily school was over by this time, or I don't think I could have done it. As it was, it cut into my fishing something terrible. I'd no sooner get out on Loon Lake in the rowboat and throw back a couple of sunfish that got caught by mistake when it would be time to cut back home and turn over that egg. And the hen would get fidgety if I stayed away too long. I guess she expected me to be right on time. I was afraid for a while that she wasn't going to stay on the job, but she did. And so did I.

I didn't know what to do about nighttime, because Mom said she didn't want me getting up in the middle of the night and Pop agreed with her. They figured it might interfere with my sleep, and maybe they were right, but I would have done it anyway. I would have done almost anything to have that egg hatch out. You don't have a chance like that every day.

Anyway, Pop said he'd turn the egg over before he went to bed at night, and if I turned it over the first thing in the

morning, then we'd leave the rest up to fate. I don't know what he meant by fate, exactly, because one night I had poison ivy on my leg and couldn't sleep very good, so I got up and went out to the henhouse to turn the egg, since I was awake anyway, and who should I meet coming out of the henhouse but Pop.

He kind of coughed in an embarrassed way, and said he couldn't get to sleep because it was so hot, so he'd just come out to see that everything was all right. I noticed it was three A.M. by the clock in the kitchen.

I asked him at breakfast if he'd been getting up every night like that. Pop poked around in his cereal bowl as if he'd found a button or something, and he said he wouldn't lose his sleep over any egg, no matter how big it was. It was only when he was awake anyway that he went out to the henhouse, he said. Mom smiled a little at the corners of her mouth, as if she thought Pop was pretty funny, but she didn't say anything.

Well, I really had my hands full. First thing in the morning I'd tear out to the hen coop and turn over the egg. By now we had the nest all fixed up in a corner of the henhouse, fenced off so it was nice and private. I'd give the hen some scratch feed and fill her water pan. Then on the way back to the house I'd take in an armful of stovewood from the shed, and by that time it would be late enough so I could bring old Ezekiel up from the cellar and put him in the chicken yard. After that I was supposed to milk the goat, but Cynthia said she'd do that for me, since the big egg was such a lot of trouble. That was pretty nice of her, I'll have to admit, because she doesn't like milking too much.

After breakfast Cynthia would help Mom in the kitchen, and I would go down to the print shop with Pop. If it was newspaper day I'd help Mr. Simmons wrap up papers for mailing, and then I'd deliver papers around town on my bike. Other days I might sweep up slugs of type lying around on the floor and melt them down in the iron pot. Then afterwards I'd pick up Joe Champigny, who lives across the street from us, and we'd go down to Loon Lake fishing. But every few hours I would come back and turn over that egg. I wasn't going to take any chances.

One morning about a week later a man came into the house and wanted to see the egg. He said he was from the newspaper in Laconia, and they wanted to run a story on this big egg that our hen had laid. I took him out to the nest, and he took some pictures and asked questions. He poked the egg with his finger and the hen nipped him. He wasn't too pleased about that, and he went off sucking his finger.

A while after that two men came from the *Christian Science Monitor,* down in Boston. They said they'd seen something in the press about a hen that laid an enormous egg up in Freedom, and they wanted to do a piece on it, because their paper was always interested in miraculous things like that. They took pictures of the egg and the hen and Ezekiel, and one of my sister feeding the chickens (as if she ever did that), and they asked all *kinds* of questions. They wanted to know why we called the rooster Ezekiel, and what the circulation of the *Freedom Sentinel* was, and how many people lived in Freedom, and all sorts of things that didn't have anything to do with the egg. Then they measured the egg with a tape, and weighed it on some hand scales they brought with them. It was fifteen inches around the narrow way, and it weighed three pounds and a quarter. The men stayed to lunch and had two helpings of pie.

The next week my Aunt Grace sent us a clipping from the *Monitor*. She lives down in Keene, and teaches high school there. The clipping had a big picture of my sister feeding the hens, and a small picture of the egg. Underneath the picture there was this article:

MAMMOTH EGG LAID IN FREEDOM

FREEDOM, N. H., June 24
Freedom, New Hampshire, may be a small town, but it sure can produce a big egg. A hen belonging to the Walter Twitchell family of this town recently laid an egg which may turn out to be the largest hen's egg in history.

Their hen laid this astonishing egg on June 16, Mr. Twitchell declared. She had shown some signs of uneasiness before laying the remarkable egg, which measures almost a foot and a half around, and weighs nearly three and a half pounds.

Mr. and Mrs. Twitchell have two children, a girl, Cynthia, 10, and a boy, Nathan, aged 12. Mr. Twitchell is the

owner and editor of the Freedom
Sentinel, a country newspaper with a
circulation of about 800. The family
has decided to let the hen sit on the
egg, in hopes that it will hatch out.
Mr. Twitchell admits that he doesn't
know what will come out of the egg,
"Something surprising," Mr. Twitchell
guesses.

Well, the three weeks were finally up. That's the time it
takes for a hen's egg to hatch out, in case you didn't know.
But nothing happened. I kept going out to the nest every little
while all day long, but nothing doing. Pop went out three
times after supper. No luck. I must have looked pretty glum,
and Mom said not to worry, maybe an egg this size needed
more time than a regular one.

A whole week went by this way, and even Mom didn't seem
to have much hope for it any more. Pop looked really discouraged. I think he'd kind of set his heart on that egg hatching out, almost as much as I had. One evening, after a whole
month had gone by, he looked at me for a while with his face
sort of screwed up.

"Nate," he said, "you counted on that egg hatching out,
didn't you?"

I said yes I had.

"And you've worked hard all this time taking care of the egg, and feeding the hen specially, and now it almost looks as if you wouldn't have anything to show for your pains, doesn't it?"

I nodded, but I didn't say anything.

He walked over to me and put his hand on my shoulder. "Well, Nate, I guess we have to expect a certain amount of hard luck every now and then, and we just have to take it. After all, it was pretty amazing just to *find* an egg like that, even if it doesn't hatch out."

"What are you going to do with it?" Mom wanted to know.

"Well, it isn't strictly fresh any more," Pop said. "I suppose we might give it to some museum. They could preserve it somehow, and put a card on it saying it was the gift of Nathan Twitchell, of Freedom, New — "

"I don't want to give it to a museum yet," I said. "I want to be sure about it first. It might be a five-week egg. You never can tell about something like this. It's not like an ordinary egg."

"But how long are you going to wait?" Cynthia said. "Are you just going to go on taking care of that old egg all summer? Remember Pop said he was going to take us camping up in Franconia Notch sometime this summer."

Pop sat down on the sofa and stretched out his legs. "Now, Nate," he said, "you deserve a lot of credit for keeping at this thing the way you have. Just don't try to follow a lost cause farther than it's worth, will you?"

"Oh no," I said. But I guess I was more disappointed than I let on. Just to myself I decided that I would give that egg one more week, and if nothing happened then — well, that would be the end of it.

Chapter Three

THAT WAS THE MOST PATIENT HEN I'D EVER
seen. She'd been sitting there on that egg for five weeks now,
and she hadn't shown any signs of giving up. I'll have to admit that I'd begun to slack off a bit on my end of the job,
and I only turned the egg over two or three times a day now,
in the morning and the evening when I went in to feed the
chickens, or sometimes at lunchtime. I was beginning to lose
interest in it, I guess, it had been so long. Besides, the weather
was so warm that I figured it didn't have to be turned so
much. Maybe the hen didn't really need to sit on it, except
nights, perhaps. But she was being so darn faithful about it
that it made me feel kind of mean to think of giving the whole
thing up before she did. After all, she wasn't complaining,
and she'd put a lot more time into it than I had.

Anyway, I had more time for fishing this way, so I didn't
mind so much. After I'd done my chores at home, and swept

out the print shop and melted down the slugs, I'd usually pick up my rod and can of bait and head for Loon Lake.

This particular morning Joe Champigny had gone down to Kezar Falls in the truck with his father for a load of lumber, and so I went down to the lake by myself. We keep our rowboat in a little sandy cove near the road, and it was such a hot morning that I slipped off my pants and shirt and had a little swim before I started fishing. I was feeling pretty good when I climbed into the boat and rowed out of the cove. Some summer people have a few cottages around the lake, and some of them were out fishing. It's just a little lake, really more of a pond, I guess, but it's got some good bass in it. I anchored out near the ledge of rocks where I generally fish. I dug out a fat old worm and baited up, and then made myself comfortable kind of leaning back on the gunwale and holding the middle part of the rod up with my toes. This sort of spreads the work around and you don't get tired in any one place first. Fish bite better if you just relax and don't try to rush them too much.

The sun sure was hot. I guess the fish were staying in the shade, because I didn't even get a nibble. After a while I got to thinking about that egg, and how disappointing it was to do all that work and not have it hatch out. I began to feel that maybe Cynthia was right. There wasn't any point in going on playing nursemaid to a freak egg all summer. But still, five weeks isn't so awfully long for a big egg like that. Some duck eggs take five weeks. That's a lot of time to put into just one egg, of course, but I guess I'd gotten a kind of funny feeling about it, and I just couldn't give up the idea that something really strange would come out of it if I just gave it time enough.

Well, after giving it a lot of thought, I decided I'd hold on for another week. That would bring it to the end of July. If nothing happened by then, I'd be willing to give that egg up as a bad job.

Just about as I'd decided that, I heard the clunk-clunk of oars bumping in oarlocks, so I lifted up the brim of my cap and looked out. Here was a little rowboat coming along towards me, with a short, sort of round-shaped man in it. He was wearing a white shirt and a white hat, the kind that summer people wear. He stopped rowing about fifty feet off and swung his boat around so he could talk to me.

"Any luck, sonny?" he asked me. He had a round red face, and his glasses were kind of on the end of his nose, which was pretty short.

I said nope.

"I suspect it's a better day for swimming than for fishing," he said.

"Yep," I said.

"Do you live around here?"

I nodded.

He didn't say anything for a while so I said, "Up in town," just to help him out. He leaned back in his boat and rested his elbows on the gunwales.

"You must know all the good fishing places then," he said, and he kind of chuckled. "But I've more sense than to ask you where they are."

He picked up a brown paper bag from the bottom of the boat and opened it up. "I think I'll have my lunch," he said. "Did you bring anything to eat?"

I shook my head.

"Do you want a ham sandwich?" he said, and he held one out for me to see it. "I don't need all this stuff. I'm too fat already."

I told him I had to go home to lunch anyway.

"That's too bad," he said. "If you had your lunch with you, you wouldn't have to go all the way back home."

"Oh, it isn't very far," I said. "And besides, I have to turn my egg over about this time."

He was just about to take a bite of his sandwich, but he stopped with it halfway to his mouth. "You have to *what?*"

"Turn my egg over," I said.

He looked at me kind of funny for a minute. "Would you mind explaining that to me?" he said. "What do you mean, *turn your egg over?*"

Well, I guess it did sound a little queer when I stopped to think of it. I couldn't help laughing a little. "Well," I said, "you see I've got this big egg that our hen laid back in June. It's a real whopper, and I've been hoping that I could hatch it out, but I have to keep turning it over because it's too big for the hen to move. I used to turn it pretty often, but I've got kind of discouraged lately about it, and only turn it three times a day."

He kept on looking at me for a while longer, and then suddenly his eyebrows went up. The wrinkles on his forehead went right under his white hat. He pointed his half-eaten sandwich at me. "Say," he said, "didn't I read about that egg in the paper some time ago? It was in the *Washington Post*, I remember, and it caught my eye because I have a collection of — of rare eggs myself. Your name must be Winchell. Was that it?"

"Twitchell," I said.

"Oh yes. Twitchell. That was it. It comes back to me now. An eighteen-inch circumference, and weighed almost four pounds."

"Three and a quarter," I said, "and only fifteen inches around."

"Yes. Very likely," he said, pushing his boat over to mine. "That's about the normal newspaper exaggeration. Now let me see, er . . . ah . . . what is your first name, anyway?"

"Nate," I said.

"Good. I'm Dr. Ziemer," he said. "All right, Nate, now when was this egg laid? Do you remember?"

"It was June sixteenth. I found it in the morning when I carried Ezekiel out of the cellar. We keep him down there because he's too noisy for the neighbors. He's our old rooster."

"Oh," Dr. Ziemer said. "I thought for a minute there that he was your grandfather. But I'm curious about this egg. What was its shape? Was it oval like an ordinary hen's egg? You know, round at one end and pointed at the other, so it won't roll out of the nest?"

"Not very. It was more long and thin, kind of like a sausage, but much bigger of course."

"I see," Dr. Ziemer said. He picked up a sandwich wrapped in wax paper and handed it to me. "Here. You eat this one. I can't digest my lunch properly with a hungry boy looking at me that way. Come on, take it."

I didn't argue about it. I was hungry enough to eat the wax paper along with it. Dr. Ziemer was chewing a mouthful of his sandwich, and it made his cheeks puff out each time he chewed.

"And what about the shell, Nate? What was that like?"

"Oh, it was kind of leathery. Not just soft-shelled the way a hen's egg is sometimes, but tough too. You can push it in a little with your finger."

One of Dr. Ziemer's eyebrows went up suddenly, but he didn't say anything. He just kept on chewing, very slowly, as if he was working on a cud or something, and he kept looking out across the lake. He did this for the longest time, and I thought he must have forgotten what we'd been talking about.

"Leathery, you say."

I nodded.

"Hmf . . . It would be impossible . . . ridiculous idea. Nonsense," he said. "Still . . ." Then he turned around and spoke to me. "Look here, Nate, would you mind taking me up to look at your egg? You see, I'm a sort of collector, in a way, and I like to look at curious specimens."

"Okay," I said.

We rowed over to the shore and tied up the boats. When

we got home, the family was eating, so I took Dr. Ziemer out
to the chicken yard. I lifted the hen off her nest, and she stood
around craning her neck to see what was going on. Dr. Ziemer
bent over with his hands on his knees, looking hard at the egg.
He felt it carefully with his finger, and then picked it up very
gently and studied it all over. He rocked it back and forth and
he even held it to his ear for a while. Finally he put it back in
the nest and pushed the straw up over it, and then he stood
up. He didn't say anything at all for a while, but just stood
there rubbing his chin and frowning down at the egg. "It's
impossible," he said.

"What is?" I asked him.

"Eh? — Oh, yes . . . Look here, Nate, are you sure you
can take good care of this egg for a while longer? You
don't think the hen is getting restless after all this time?
The sixteenth of June it was laid, didn't you say? Now let me

see . . ." He took a little calendar out of his pocket. "That makes five weeks day before yesterday. Six weeks on the twenty-eighth. Nate, may I speak to your father about this?"

I took him in and introduced him to the family. Dr. Ziemer bowed to my mother and Cynthia, and shook Pop's hand. "Very pleased to meet you, Mr. Winchell," he said.

"Twitchell," I reminded him.

"Oh, yes, yes. Twitchell, of course. I'm very sorry. Mr. Twitchell, your boy has a very remarkable egg out there, and I think there is a chance that it may hatch. Possibly within a week — "

" You do? " Pop said.

Dr. Ziemer held up his hand. "A chance, mind you. I don't want to raise your hopes unduly. But I think there is a chance. There isn't any danger it will be disturbed? No dogs or any-thing like that? It's such an unusual egg, you see, it would be a pity to have anything happen to it."

Pop smiled. "It's been there more than a month, and noth-ing's bothered it so far."

"Yes. So far. But we'd want to be sure that nothing would bother it *after* it hatches. You see, it might turn out to be . . . well, of an unusual appearance, you know."

"I see," Pop said. He gave Dr. Ziemer a kind of a funny look. "We might put some extra wire around the nest. That would make it safe."

"Good, good. And one more thing. Would you please call me if it hatches? I'm staying with the MacPhersons, down at the lake. Just call me as soon as it hatches, no matter what time of day."

"Glad to, Dr. Ziemer," Pop said. "But have you any idea what it may turn out to be?"

"It *might* turn out to be almost anything. I'd hardly dare guess. I wouldn't want to even suggest what I think it is. You'd think I was crazy. But I must go along and let you finish your lunch. I'll be waiting to hear from you. Good-by."

We all stood at the door and watched him going down the road. When we were all sitting at the table again, Pop looked across at me and said, "What do you suppose he meant by 'an unusual appearance'?"

"Search me," I said.

Chapter Four

THAT NEXT WEEK WENT BY AWFULLY SLOWLY. I went out to look at the egg about every half hour, I guess. After what Dr. Ziemer had said about the egg maybe hatching, I was getting pretty anxious to see what was going to happen. But every time I looked in the nest, the egg was just lying there, just as it had for a month and a half. The hen was beginning to look kind of bored too, as if she didn't really care any more whether the old thing hatched out or not. That was a bad sign, because this was no time to quit, just when the end was in sight. If the hen had walked off the job now, I think I would have sat on the egg myself.

Well, Saturday came around at last, but no news from the egg. I'd been out to see it so many times that morning that Mom had said, "A watched pot never boils, Nate." I never could figure out how grownups could be so *patient* about things all the time. We were having dinner, and I could hardly sit still.

Pop had been looking at me for a while. "You know, Nate," he said, "you don't want to get your heart set on this thing too much. If you get too eager about it, you're going to be awfully hard hit if that old thing doesn't hatch. I kind of suspect we're running on borrowed time anyway. I never heard of an egg that took more than *five* weeks."

"But Dr. Ziemer said it might hatch within a week."

"And who is Dr. Ziemer?" Mom wanted to know. "Just because he's a doctor, that doesn't mean he knows everything. Why, a city doctor like him probably doesn't know the first thing about poultry."

"That's right, Nate," Pop said. "He's probably a big eye, ear, nose and throat man from New York or Philadelphia. Chances are he's a specialist on the inner ear, or something like that, and hasn't been called to look at a sick egg since he was in medical school."

Cynthia giggled. "I can just see him asking the egg to stick out its tongue and say 'Ah.' "

I didn't see anything very funny. After all, if you've taken care of something for all that time you don't feel too much like joking about it. "But Dr. Ziemer talked as if he knew a lot about it," I said. "He said he collected eggs, or something like that."

"So do we," Pop said. "We collect them twice a day."

"Besides," Mom said, "this one is something new. I don't

imagine he's seen anything like this before. How could he know what it's likely to do?"

Pop grinned. "Don't know that you could call a six-week egg exactly *new*. Except compared with a dinosaur egg, perhaps. Maybe Dr. Ziemer collects dinosaur eggs."

"Now Walt, don't be ridiculous," Mom said. "Just stop talking, everybody, and finish up. I've got a berry pie for dessert. They're the blueberries that Cynthia picked Thursday up in Thompson's meadow." She went over to the stove and brought the pie out of the oven. She put the bread board down on the table and set the pie down on it. A little shiny trickle of blueberry juice had leaked out through a hole in the crust, and you could just see that good warm smell coming out.

"Dinosaur eggs, indeed!" Mom said.

We didn't say much until after the pie was all gone. After dinner I went out to look at the egg again, but nothing doing.

Nothing doing at suppertime either, or at bedtime. In the evening Pop talked a lot about going camping in Franconia Notch. I guess he was trying to get my mind off the egg, and to tell the truth, I was kind of getting ready to ease myself over a pretty stiff disappointment that I felt was coming. When I went upstairs to bed, I tried to persuade myself that it wouldn't have been so much even if the egg had hatched out. Perhaps just triplet chicks, or something, and they probably wouldn't have lived anyway.

In the morning I crawled out of bed feeling pretty gloomy about things. I was trying to fasten my mind on the camping trip so I wouldn't think about the egg any more. I went down to the cellar and got old Ezekiel out of his box. As usual, he flapped his wings and clawed around a lot, and I stumbled up the cellar stairs with his wing feathers in my face. I tripped over a bucket and mop that somebody had left at the top of the stairs, and Ezekiel got loose and made a couple of trips around the kitchen before I could herd him out the door. By the time I got him out to the chicken yard I was about ready to give up everything that had anything to do with chickens or eggs or anything like that.

That was probably why I didn't notice anything different at first. I just went over to the nest and put a little grain down for that poor old hen, and started to turn away, when I realized all at once that something had changed. The hen wasn't sitting on the nest any more. She was walking back and forth with a kind of wild look in her eye, and every time she came near the nest she gave a little hop and fluttered away again. I bent down to look in the nest, and — *wow!* There was something in there, and it was alive! It was moving around.

I thought at first that it was a rat or something that had busted the egg and eaten it. But after I got a good look I could see that it wasn't any rat. It was about the size of a squirrel, but it didn't have any hair, and its head — well, I

couldn't believe my eyes when I saw it. It didn't look like anything I'd ever seen before. It had three little knobs sticking out of its head and a sort of collar up over its neck. It was a lizardy-looking critter, and it kept moving its thick tail slowly back and forth in the nest. The poor hen was looking pretty upset. I guess she hadn't expected anything like this, and neither had I.

I just stood there for a minute; I was so surprised all I could do was look. Then I started yelling, and lit out across the yard as fast as I could go. When I busted into the kitchen Mom was so startled that she dropped a saucepan in the sink. Pop came running down the stairs with lather over one side of his face and a razor in his hand, and Cynthia was right behind.

"For goodness' sakes!" Mom said. "What's the matter with you?"

"It's alive!" I shouted. "It's alive! And it moves around, and it wiggles its tail and has horns and it looks like a lizard, and it doesn't have any fur, and the hen's running round and round and doesn't know what to do about it, and — "

"Hold on there, Nate," Pop said. "You look as if you'd seen a ghost. What's all the excitement about?"

I was so out of breath that I couldn't talk for a while. "It's the egg" I said. "It's hatched!"

"*What!*" Pop shouted. "It did? Why didn't you say so?" And he ran out the door and down the steps, still holding on to his razor. I grabbed Mom's hand and pulled her along, and Cynthia was just ahead of us. She'd forgotten to put on her shoes, and Mom was saying, "All this excitement over an egg. My goodness!"

When we all got out to the nest, Pop was leaning over, looking hard at it. Mom was still saying, "Why we should all come running out here only half dressed, just to see an egg that hatched out — I can't see anything in there, it's too dark. Walt, why don't you bring it out here so we can look at it, whatever it is?"

Pop was still leaning over staring at that thing in the nest. All he said was, "By jing!" under his breath, sort of. By that time Cynthia had squeezed in beside Pop. She took one good look and then let out a screech that you could have heard way down to the post office. That started the hen off, and she began squawking and flapping around in circles, and Ezekiel started crowing, and the goat started bleating. There was an awful lot of commotion, and everybody was talking at the same time and nobody could hear anything.

When it quieted down a little, Pop said, "Nate, you better run into the house and call Dr. Ziemer. He wanted to be told first thing. Remember, he's at the MacPhersons' place."

When I got hold of the operator on the telephone, I asked her to ring the MacPhersons, but she said it was only half-past six and that was pretty early to call those summer people. "Are you sure you can't wait till later?" Mrs. Beebe wanted to know. She's the operator, and she knows just about everybody in town by their voices.

"Well, it's sort of an emergency," I told her. "It's for Dr. Ziemer — he's staying at the MacPhersons', and he told me to call him the minute the egg hatched, and — "

"Oh, did your egg hatch, Nate?" said Mrs. Beebe. "Well, now, isn't that nice. What was in it?"

"Oh, gosh, Mrs. Beebe, it was pretty strange, but you'd better ring the MacPhersons, because Dr. Ziemer wanted me to call him right away, just as soon as the egg hatched."

"All right, Nate, I'll ring their number. But those folks come from Washington, and they don't hardly ever get up this early down there."

I could hear her ring the number, and it rang and rang for quite a while before anybody answered. Finally somebody picked up the receiver and said, "Hello?" in a kind of husky voice.

"Can I speak to Dr. Ziemer?" I said.

"Dr. Ziemer? He's sleeping. Who is this anyway?" the voice said.

"This is Nate Twitchell. Dr. Ziemer said to call him right away when the egg hatched, no matter what time it was."

"When the *egg* hatched? Say, what are you talking about?"

"Well," I explained, "we have this egg up here, and Dr. Ziemer wanted to see what was in it when it hatched, and it has. He acted like it was pretty important. He said he collected eggs."

"Oh," the voice said, "he said that? Collected eggs, eh? That's a good one. Well, okay, I'll tell him, but it's awfully early. Just hold on a minute, will you?"

There was a long silence on the other end of the line, and then I heard the receiver picked up again.

"Hello there, Nate. That you?"

"Yes, Dr. Ziemer. The egg finally hatched out."

"It did? Is it alive?"

"Sure is," I said.

"What's it look like, Nate? Can you describe it?"

"Well, it's a queer-looking thing. Looks like a big lizard, except that it's got little horns on the — "

There was a kind of whoop on the other end of the phone, and Dr. Ziemer yelled, "I'll be right over," and then there was a crashing sound, as if he'd forgotten to let go of the receiver.

Chapter Five

Dr. ZIEMER ARRIVED WHILE WE WERE STILL staring at the thing in the nest. He jumped out of his car and came running out to us in the back yard. He was wearing a red bathrobe over his pajamas, and he looked pretty excited.

He ran up to the nest and looked in. His eyes opened up wide and he knelt down on the ground and stared and stared and stared. After a long while he said softly, "That's it. By George, that's just what it is." Then he stared for another long time and finally he shook his head and said, "It can't be true, but there it is."

He got up off his knees and looked around at us. His eyes were just sparkling, he was so excited. He put his hand on my shoulder, and I could feel he was quivering. "An amazing thing's happened," he said, in a kind of whisper. "I don't know how to account for it. It must be some sort of freak biological mixup that might happen once in a thousand years."

"But what is it?" I asked.

Dr. Ziemer turned and pointed a trembling finger at the nest. "Believe it or not, you people have hatched out a *dinosaur*."

We just looked at him.

"Sounds incredible, I know," he said, "and I can't explain it, but there it is. I've seen too many Triceratops skulls to be mistaken about this one."

"But — but how could it be a dinosaur?" Pop asked.

"Goodness gracious!" Mom spluttered. "And right here in our back yard. It doesn't seem hardly right. And on a Sunday, too."

Cynthia was pretty interested by now, and kept peeking into the nest and making faces, the way she did when Pop brought a bowl of frogs' legs into the kitchen one time. I guess girls just naturally don't like crawly things too much. To tell the truth, I don't either sometimes, but this thing that had just hatched out looked kind of cute to me. Maybe that was because I had taken care of the egg so long. I felt as if the little dinosaur was almost one of the family.

We stood around for a long while looking at the strange new thing on the nest, trying to let the idea soak in that we had a dinosaur. After Dr. Ziemer calmed down a little, he and Pop tightened up the chicken wire to make sure the little animal wasn't going to crawl out. Dr. Ziemer watched the poor old hen for a time, and then he wondered if perhaps she ought not to be taken out before she went out of her mind. Pop figured that it might be a good idea and he picked her up and put her outside the pen. She acted a little dazed at first, but pretty soon she followed the other hens and began scratching for worms like the rest of them.

"I've never seen such a surprised hen in my life," Dr. Ziemer said.

Mom suddenly began to notice how we all looked. "Cynthia, you're still in your pajamas!" she said. "You get right into the house and get dressed. Walt, you've only shaved half your face. My goodness! The neighbors will think we're crazy. And we haven't had breakfast yet! What am I thinking of? Dr. Ziemer, won't you stay and have breakfast with us?"

Dr. Ziemer said, "Why, yes, thank you very much." And then he happened to look at his bathrobe. "But I'm not dressed myself."

"Oh, that's all right," Pop told him. "This is no time to worry about clothes. We always wear bathrobes when our dinosaurs hatch."

Dr. Ziemer laughed, and we all went back in the house. Mom got a big breakfast, and we all tucked into the bacon and eggs and hot biscuits and honey as if we'd been starving.

Afterwards Dr. Ziemer leaned back and patted his stomach. "I haven't had a breakfast like this in years," he said. "Those biscuits are worth coming miles for, Mrs. Twitchell."

"You probably don't have a chance to eat a decent meal without being interrupted," Mom said to him. "A doctor's life must be terribly hard, with emergency calls all the time, day and night."

Dr. Ziemer looked at her, sort of surprised. "You know," he said, "I think you've got me in the wrong profession. I'm not a *medical* doctor. I'm a paleontologist. My patients have all been dead for fifty million years or so." I saw him wink at Pop.

Cynthia's mouth dropped open. "Fifty million — " she said. "Say, what is a paleo — paleon — well, whatever it is you just said?"

Dr. Ziemer looked at me. "Do you know, Nate?"

"Well, no," I said. "Not exactly." I could hear Cynthia snicker at me.

"A paleontologist is someone who is interested in very ancient life," Dr. Ziemer said. "He goes around trying to find old bones and fossil remains of plants and animals so he can know what kinds of things lived long ago. Actually, I should call myself a paleozoologist, because I'm particularly interested in animal life, like dinosaurs, for example. That was why I was very anxious to see what came out of this egg of Nate's."

"Well, I *never*," Mom said. "So that's why you thought that the egg might hatch out."

"I certainly hoped it would, anyway," Dr. Ziemer said. "You see, all we've had to work on so far is fossils, just bones, teeth, footprints, and so forth. Naturally, we haven't been able to be sure about many things, because up to today nobody has ever seen a live dinosaur. As a matter of fact, no one was even sure that dinosaurs hatched out of eggs until Roy Chapman Andrews found some dinosaur eggs in the Gobi Desert in 1923. So you see, this dinosaur in your back yard here is tremendously important and scientists all over the world are going to be grateful to Nate and his family for taking care of such a valuable egg." Dr. Ziemer had been talking so much that he had forgotten about the biscuit he held in his hand, but now he broke it open and put a dab of butter on it. He looked around the kitchen and frowned a little. "This is such a nice peaceful place, you know. But now the trouble begins. When the news gets around, the scientific world is going to go crazy. I'm afraid it may change things quite a bit around here. Science has done an enormous amount of good for the human race. But it rarely makes things any more peaceful. When I send a telegram to my colleagues at the National Museum saying that I have seen a *live* Triceratops, they're going to take the first plane out of Washington. If they believe me, that is. Then there will be an official announcement to the press and right after that there will be crowds of scientists and other inquisitive people from all over and there will be a big hullabaloo. It will make your quiet little back yard look like Union Station. People will be coming and going, and stepping in your flower beds, and leaving cigarette wrappers all around. I hate to upset your lives here that way."

"Well, now, do we have to tell anybody that we've got a dinosaur?" Mom said. "I don't see why it's anybody's business but our own."

Dr. Ziemer smiled and shook his head. "They'd find out anyway, Mrs. Twitchell, whether we told them or not. And besides, I owe it to my colleagues to tell them about anything I discover. I expect them to do the same for me. We scientists don't like to keep secrets from each other. We're just not made that way."

"We could send it away to a museum, or a zoo," Cynthia said. "Then all those crowds of paleo-people could hang around the museum and they wouldn't bother us at all."

Dr. Ziemer looked around at me. "How about it, Nate? Would you let your dinosaur go to a museum? I could take him to the National Museum in Washington, where I work. I would promise to take the very best care of him."

"But I wouldn't get to see him then," I said. "I don't think I'd like that too much. I'm not a scientist, but I'm kind of interested in him too. You don't get a chance to have a dinosaur of your own very often, you know."

"Well, I can't say I blame you, Nate," Dr. Ziemer said. "But I really feel that I have to tell the other scientists about this. What will we do?"

"I tell you what," Pop said. "I think Nate's got the right to keep the dinosaur if he went to all that trouble to hatch it out. And I guess the doctor has a responsibility to tell the world what he knows, so it looks as if Dr. Ziemer had better go ahead and send his telegram, and the rest of us will brace ourselves for the shock as best we can. Maybe we can figure out some way to work it so that we won't be completely swamped."

"Now let me see," Dr. Ziemer said, rubbing his chin. "How would this be? We could make some rules about visiting hours, say from eight in the morning until suppertime, or whatever you like, and then let in just a few people at a time to avoid crowding. Then there's the telephone. I don't know what you could do about that. That can be an awful nuisance, if it rings all day and night."

"Oh, Mrs. Beebe can take care of that," Mom said. "She can tell them to wait until morning if they call at night. She's very good at that."

"And I could answer the phone in the daytime," Cynthia said. "I could be a kind of secretary. It would be fun. When the phone rang, I'd pick up the receiver and say, 'Good morning. This is Mr. Twitchell's residence.' And then I'd write down their names and all that. And it would be very good experience for me, wouldn't it, Mom?"

"And I could be the keeper," I said. "I would say 'Step this way, ladies and gentlemen. Watch out for the petunias there, sir. This is the only living Tric — er — ty — only living dinosaur in the world, and — "

"Only *known* living dinosaur, Nate," Dr. Ziemer said. "We must be scientific about this, of course." He turned to Cynthia. "All right, then, young lady, here's your first job. Got a pencil and paper?"

She grabbed the pencil and pad from the telephone box and sat down again.

"All set?" Dr. Ziemer said. "I'd like you to send this wire collect to Alfred Kennedy, United States National Museum, Washington, D. C." He waited while Cynthia wrote this down and then he said, "Have day-old Triceratops alive. Come quick. Signed Ziemer." He could see Cynthia was having quite a bit of trouble with "Triceratops," so he spelled that out for her. Then he leaned back and chuckled to himself. "I

wish I could see Kennedy's face when he reads that. Well, I must go back and get dressed. We'll probably have a few hours before things start popping. I'll come back after dinner, Nate, and we'll work up some sort of pen for that animal of yours and we can give him a little food. Thank you all very much for the breakfast."

When he had gone, Mom began bustling around. "Hurry up, Cynthia, and send off that telegram. Then while you're doing the dishes I'll straighten up upstairs. Nate, you better go out and milk the goat and then get washed and put on your good suit. We've only got three quarters of an hour before church."

"Oh, do we *have* to go to church today, Mom?" I said. "I've got an awful lot to do for that dinosaur before people start coming to look at it. I should think we could skip church just this once when such an important thing has happened. Dr. Ziemer said the scientific world's going to go crazy, didn't he?"

"Never mind that," Mom said. "There's no reason to give up going to church just because we've got a dinosaur out back. Get a move on, now."

Chapter Six

AFTER CHURCH I SAW JOE CHAMPIGNY OUT in his back yard. I went over to talk to him.

"Hey, Joe," I said. "Guess what hatched out of my egg."

"A duck?" Joe asked.

"Nope."

"A turkey?"

"Nope. I'll give you a hint. It's got four legs."

Joe looked at me and wrinkled up his face. "Two ducks?"

I could see that he wasn't going to get anywhere that way, so I told him. "It's a *dinosaur*. A real little live dinosaur. What do you think of *that?*"

"Ah, go on," Joe said. "Who are you kidding?"

"*Honest* it is. Come on over and look at it. It's got little horns on its face and everything."

We went across the street into our back yard, and squatted down by the dinosaur nest. Joe didn't see him at first, but then

his eyes got accustomed to the dark. "Jeepers, it's a big lizard!" he said, kind of drawing back a little. "You mean that all came out of that egg? Is he poisonous? He sure looks poisonous to me."

"I don't know," I said. I hadn't thought of that before. I'd have to ask Dr. Ziemer about it. He didn't *seem* poisonous.

"What you going to feed him?" Joe wanted to know.

"I don't know that either," I said. "But I'll find out, and then I'll tame him, and he'll be about the only pet dinosaur in the whole world, I bet."

"That's no dinosaur," Joe Champigny said. "It's just a big lizard. Where'd you get the idea it was a dinosaur, anyway?"

"Dr. Ziemer said it was, and he's a paleo — something, and he works in a museum and knows all about dinosaurs and things like that. Really, he does. He knew the egg was going to hatch out, and he knew what kind of an egg it was, too."

Joe put his hands on his hips and shook his head slowly back and forth. "You know what I think?" he said. "He's just making fun of you. These summer people think they're awful smart, and they think that just because we live up here in Freedom, New Hampshire, we don't know anything. They think we're all suckers for jokes like this. That's what my dad says."

Just then we heard Joe's mother calling him. "Jeepers," Joe said. "I forgot all about the stovewood. See you later."

I didn't agree with what Joe said about Dr. Ziemer. He didn't look like the kind of man who'd play a trick like that. And he looked too excited when he first saw the thing. And he sent a telegram to Washington too. Or at least he had us send one.

After dinner Dr. Ziemer drove up in his car. He walked out to the back yard, where I was sitting watching the dinosaur. "Hello there, Nate," he said. "How is our little freak? Still lively?" He bent down and looked inside the box to make sure for himself. "Yes, sir, he looks fine. Probably hungry too. We'd better get him his first meal, Nate."

"What does he eat?" I said. "Do we have to feed him milk out of a baby's bottle?"

Dr. Ziemer laughed at that. "Oh no, Nate, we don't have to bottle-feed a dinosaur. You see, dinosaurs are reptiles, like snakes and turtles, and when they hatch out of the egg, they're all ready to eat the same kind of food that adults eat. The kind of dinosaur the Triceratops is is a grass-eater, so all we have to do is keep him supplied with grass, or leaves, or lily pads or lettuce — and a few small pebbles every now and then."

"Pebbles?" I said. "Does he eat pebbles?"

Dr. Ziemer smiled. "What kind of teeth does a chicken have, Nate?"

"Doesn't have teeth," I said. "They just have little stones in their gizzard — say, do you mean a dinosaur has a gizzard like a chicken?"

"Some of them do. When scientists dug up dinosaur bones they sometimes found a pile of smooth stones right in the middle of the dinosaur skeleton. They didn't know what they were at first, until it suddenly dawned on them that they were gizzard stones. Some of the stones were as big as a man's fist."

"Seems funny for an animal to have a gizzard," I said.

"No funnier than for a chicken to have one, is it? Well, let's try him out on some grass and some leaves, and see which he likes better."

We picked some maple leaves from the tree in the yard, and I got a handful of grass from outside the fence. We put them down in two piles, grass in one, and leaves in the other, and we carefully put the nest box on its side so the dinosaur could come out if he wanted to. Then we sat down and watched. The little dinosaur saw the piles of food, I guess, because he started right out for them. His legs looked kind of weak at first, and he stumbled around a little. When he came out into the sunshine he blinked, but he kept right on going. The first pile he came to was the grass. He put his head right down into that green grass and started swallowing away at it.

"I guess he likes grass, all right," I said. The little fellow kept right on swallowing until the handful of grass was all

gone. All that was left was a blade of grass hanging out of the corner of his mouth which he hadn't noticed yet. Then he wobbled over to the pile of leaves and started in on that.

"I guess he likes leaves too," Dr. Ziemer said. "Look at him eat, will you? He's just about finished it up already."

I ran over and got some more grass, and another handful of leaves. "Put them all together in one pile," Dr. Ziemer said, "and then we'll see what he picks out first."

But he didn't stop to pick things out. He just ate his way through the pile, and when it was all gone he stood on three legs and scratched his neck with a hind foot. Then he walked over to a smooth sunny place and lay down.

"Well," Dr. Ziemer said, "with an appetite like that, he's going to have us humping to keep him supplied with food.

Too bad we can't put him in the pasture. But he's too small for that. He'd crawl through the fence, or maybe the goat would hurt him."

"She's a very gentle goat," I said. "She wouldn't even hurt a kitten."

"Maybe not a kitten, but a dinosaur is something different. Animals can get excited when they see something they haven't come across before. So can people, I guess. We'd better wait till this little fellow gets bigger before we put him in the pasture. By the way, we ought to be keeping a record of his growth. Do you happen to have some scales in the house?"

"Sure. We have some in the kitchen. Mom doesn't ever use them. Shall we carry him in and weigh him?"

"Well, perhaps it would be better policy to bring the scales out here," Dr. Ziemer said. "Women often have a prejudice against reptiles, you know, and we wouldn't want to cause any trouble. See if you can borrow the scales for a while."

I ran in and got the scales. When I told Mom what they were for, she said I could keep the scales outside. She didn't want to have anything in her kitchen that "that creature" had touched. I guess Dr. Ziemer was right.

We put the scales down on the ground, and I went over to pick up the animal. He had a bluish skin like a lizard's, and a funny kind of a beak, something like a snapping turtle has.

Of course he didn't have that mean look like a snapper, but you can't ever be sure. I stood there for a moment looking at him. I wasn't scared to pick him up, but you see I'd never handled a dinosaur before, and I didn't know much about how to do it.

Dr. Ziemer was watching me. "What's the matter, Nate? Does he look dangerous?"

"I was just studying how I ought to get a hold of him," I said. "He has a kind of sharp-looking mouth, and I'd just as soon not get my hand nipped. What do *you* think?"

"Well, to tell the truth, I've never had to deal with any of these fellows when they were alive. My dinosaurs have all been just piles of old bones, and they never even *tried* to bite me." He came over and stood beside me. "Let's just see how touchy he is." He put his foot out and gently poked one of the dinosaur's feet. The dinosaur sat up and looked around. He was pretty sleepy.

"He looks rather calm and amiable," the doctor said. "Would you like me to pick him up first this time?"

As a matter of fact, I wasn't too eager to catch hold of him, but somehow I thought I ought to be the one to pick him up first, since he *was* my dinosaur and all. Besides, I didn't want Dr. Ziemer to think that I was really scared or anything. So I said, "No thanks, I'll pick him up."

"All right, Nate. I'd suggest you hold him just back of the

front legs. He has a short neck, and I don't think he could reach you that way. Be easy, now. We don't want to frighten him."

I reached down slowly, and slid my hands around his body. He wriggled a little, but didn't try to bite. His skin felt all warm and sort of slidy and loose. When he seemed to be used to my hands being there, I picked him up slowly and set him down on the kitchen scales. He kicked a few times while he was in the air, but he settled down again when he was on the scales. He lay there quietly, with his thick tail hanging over the edge. I guess he just wanted to sleep.

We looked at the dial on the scales, and it said four and a quarter pounds. The doctor wrote that down in a little notebook.

"Of course," he said, "this is not his original weight. We'll have to approximate that. We'll gather as much grass and leaves as we had before, as close as we can estimate it, and then we'll weigh that and see how much he's eaten."

We gathered the grass and leaves, and it weighed just a little over a pound.

"Your baby's got a good appetite," the doctor said. "He put away over a third of his own weight. Let's see now, that means that he weighed approximately three pounds when hatched." He wrote that down in his notebook. "And now for his length." He took a tape measure out of his pocket. "Set him down on the ground, would you, Nate?"

I lifted him down on the ground again, and we stretched out his tail and measured him from tip to tip. Thirteen and a half inches, he was. The doctor wrote that down, and then measured his head, and the length of his tail, and his legs, and he wrote the measurements down each time in his notebook. He was awfully careful about it.

"What kind of a dinosaur did you say this was?" I asked him.

"Triceratops," he said, measuring a hind leg. "Let's see, four point five inches, pelvis to metatarsals."

"Is a Tricerapops poisonous, Dr. Zeimer?" I asked him.

"No sir, Nate. These fellows had too much armor to need poison. Femur, two inches — no, one point seven five — I'm not accustomed to working on bones with the skin on. Do you think I'd ask you to pick him up if I thought he was poisonous? Tibia, two inches . . ." He was going on at a great rate.

"How big does the Tricerapops get to be?" I asked when he was finished.

"Sometimes more than twenty feet. And it's Tricera*tops*, not *pops*, my boy."

"Twenty *feet!*" I said. "You mean twenty inches, don't you?"

"No, I mean twenty feet. That includes the tail, of course. They might weigh up to ten tons or so at full size."

"Ten tons!" I almost fell over backward with surprise. "My gosh, think of all the grass it would take to feed him. How long does it take him to get that big?" I was pretty worried, because anything *that* big would eat up all of Mrs. Parson's grass in just one day, I should think.

"Oh, it would take a good long time, I'm sure. The fact is, though, we don't really *know* much about how fast these animals grew because we've never had any live ones before. We know about their size, all right, because we've found their skeletons, but we don't know how long it took them to reach full size, or how long they lived, or their rate of growth. That's why we must keep careful records on this little fellow. Science is going to be very interested."

Just then I heard the screen door slam at the back of the house, and Cynthia came running out with a paper in her hand.

"Dr. Ziemer!" she called. "There's a telegram for you. It's from Washington. It came on the telephone, and I wrote it down."

She gave the paper to the doctor. He looked at it, and his eyebrows went up and down a couple of times while he read it.

"I had to write it pretty fast," Cynthia said, "so my handwriting wasn't too good."

"Oh pshaw!" the doctor said. "The old skeptic. Here, Nate, read this." And he handed me the paper.

I read it. Cynthia wasn't kidding about the handwriting. It was about all I could do to make it out.

DOCTOR OSCAR ZIEMER CARE OF WALTER TWITCHELL FREE-DOM NEW HAMPSHIRE. QUIT COMEDY ZIEMER YOU BUFFOON. TOO HOT HERE FOR JOKES. KENNEDY.

"Well, how do you like that?" the doctor said. "The old fool! He never has trusted me since I put the beef bone in his Paleoscincus collection. Come on, Cynthia, let's go call him up and tell him to get a move on, or we'll give the news to the Museum of Natural History. That will bring him all right."

They went into the house, and I sat down under the maple

tree in the shade. It was awfully hot in the sun. Pretty soon Joe Champigny came along and sat down with me.

"How's your lizard, Nate?" he said.

"It's no lizard, it's a dinosaur."

"I betcha it isn't. I asked my pop about it, and he said there wasn't any such thing as dinosaurs. He said nobody ever saw any. Some crazy scientists found a lot of old bones and they just made up all that business about dinosaurs out of their heads."

"There were too dinosaurs." I said. "Just because nobody's seen them doesn't mean there weren't any, and besides if there weren't any dinosaurs, how come I've got one right here?"

"Fooey, that's no dinosaur," Joe said.

"It is too. It's a Triceraclops, or something like that, and if a Triceraclops isn't a dinosaur, I'd like to know what *is*."

"Fooey," Joe Champigny said.

Sometimes Joe's an awfully hard guy to argue with.

Chapter Seven

DR. ZIEMER CAME OUT THE BACK DOOR.

"There," he said. "I guess that will bring Dr. Kennedy all right. I called him up and said that if he wasn't here by noon tomorrow, I'd have to consult the paleontologists at the Museum of Natural History. I finally convinced him that I wasn't fooling, and he said he'd take a plane out of Washington as soon as he could."

He walked over and sat down in the shade with us under the maple tree. Pretty soon Cynthia brought out a tray with four glasses of lemonade, and we all sat around sipping the lemonade very slowly, to make it last longer.

"It's nice and quiet here now," Dr. Ziemer said. "I suppose we might as well enjoy it while we can. In another twenty-four hours or so I suspect things are really going to be popping in Freedom."

"And I guess I'll be very busy answering phone calls," Cynthia said. "I suppose there will be some from a long way off, like Boston and Portland. That will be exciting. I like to think of those voices coming along all those miles of wire all the way from Boston."

"Even farther than that, I bet," I said. "Maybe even from New York. Even Chicago, maybe."

"Oh go on, Nate," Joe Champigny said. "Who would ever hear about your lizard in Chicago? That's way out west in Ohio."

"It isn't either in Ohio," I said. "It's in Michigan or some place like that. Anyway, not in Ohio. And it's not a lizard," I said. "It's a dinosaur, I tell you. Ask Dr. Ziemer."

"Looks like a lizard to me," Joe said.

Dr. Ziemer swirled his lemonade around to stir up the sugar in the bottom of the glass. He looked over at Joe with his eyebrows up and sort of smiled to himself. "It is a *kind* of lizard," he said. "That's what the word *dinosaur* means — a terrible lizard."

"But how come a dinosaur would come out of a hen's egg?" Joe wanted to know. "That doesn't make sense."

Dr. Ziemer shrugged his shoulders. "You've got me there," he said. "That's the queer thing about this. Of course Nature does play tricks every now and then. Sometimes a calf is born with three legs, or a chicken hatches out with webbed feet like a duck's. Sometimes an animal will inherit something from an ancestor way back along the family tree somewhere. If I had red hair, for instance, and no one else in my family had it, everyone would wonder where the red hair came from, and then they would find out that my great-great-grandmother had red hair, and I had inherited it from her. Do you see that?"

We all nodded.

"Well," the doctor said, "if you go back far enough, and I mean millions of years, you'll find that birds and reptiles are related to each other. That's why they are alike in some ways. How is a chicken like a turtle, for example?"

"A chicken like a turtle?" I looked at Joe and he looked back at me. Neither of us could think of anything.

"They both lay eggs," Cynthia said.

Well, Joe and I both felt pretty silly about that. How did my sister ever think of that? I didn't know that she'd ever even looked at a turtle. I guess girls notice things more than you'd think.

"That's right," said Dr. Ziemer. "They both lay eggs."

Joe looked up suddenly. "A turtle's got a scaly kind of skin, and chickens are sort of scaly on their legs."

"Good for you, Joe," the doctor said.

"And neither of them have teeth," I said.

Dr. Ziemer nodded. "So you see," he said, "birds are like reptiles in some ways. And dinosaurs are reptiles. What must have happened here is that things got a bit mixed up, and when the egg hatched out, it turned out to be another branch

of the family. That isn't a very scientific explanation, but I'm rather puzzled by this myself. It's a very peculiar thing."

Joe Champigny looked at him for a while. "But I thought you were a scientist," he said. "Scientists are supposed to know all the answers, aren't they? Like teachers?"

Dr. Ziemer smiled and shook his head. "No, Joe, a scientist doesn't know all the answers. Nobody does, not even teachers. But a scientist keeps on trying to find the answers."

He stood up and dusted off the knees of his pants. "Well, I guess I ought to go back to the MacPhersons'. They'll be wondering what has happened to me. Nate, you probably should give your dinosaur another meal of grass some time later today. I'll be over in the morning in time to greet Dr. Kennedy when he gets here."

I went out to feed the chickens before supper. On the way I got a big armful of grass and put it in the dinosaur's pen. He came waddling out of the box and started right in on the grass. He was still going strong when Mom called me in to supper.

"Have you given your animal a name, Nate?" Pop wanted to know.

"Not yet," I said. "Got any suggestions?"

"Well, I don't know," Pop said slowly. "I've sacrificed most of my best family names to the livestock by now. Perhaps there's a good name on your mother's side of the family.

Seems to me there was . . . now, what *was* his name? It was your great-uncle, wasn't it?"

"Oh," Mom said. "You must be thinking of Great-uncle John Beazley."

"That's it!" Pop said. "You could shorten it to Uncle Beazley, I should think, and come to think of it, if I recollect his picture, there is a certain resemblance between the two —"

"Walter!" Mom said. "Great-uncle Beazley was a very good man. He just got a bit crotchety along toward the end. I don't think we should say anything disrespectful of him."

"Why, not at all," Pop said. "It really is more of an honor. It may be that the name of Uncle Beazley will go down in history if we name this young dinosaur after him."

"Hmmf," Mom said, with a little smile.

"Uncle Beazley . . . Uncle Beazley . . . Uncle Beazley . . ." I said, sort of trying it out. Cynthia giggled.

"All right," I said. "It sounds pretty good after you get used to it. I guess I'll take it if Mom doesn't mind."

After supper I went out to see how things were. The grass was all gone, every bit of it, and the little fellow was lying down in his box. I could just see him there in the dark. I really had gotten to like him a lot already.

"Good night, Uncle Beazley," I said, and went back into the house.

Chapter Eight

IT WASN'T LONG AFTER BREAKFAST THE NEXT morning when there was a loud knock on the front door. I went to answer it. There was a tall thin man standing there with a kind of a small suitcase. He looked sort of annoyed.

"Dr. Ziemer in?"

"No," I said. "He doesn't live here."

"Well, where does he live? This is Walter Twitchell's house, isn't it?"

"Yes, but Dr. Ziemer doesn't live here. He's staying at the MacPhersons'."

"MacPhersons'? Where the devil is that?"

I pointed down the road to the right. "You go down that road about a half a mile until you come to the forks. Take the right hand road there — I mean the one that goes *sharp* right — the middle road takes you over to Kezar Falls. Then follow that road for — well, for a ways, and pretty soon you'll come to a sharp curve where there's a barway in a stone wall, but the bars are all down 'cause they don't keep cows in there any more — "

"Oh, they don't, eh?" the tall man said. "Isn't that fascinating, now?" I thought he sounded kind of impatient.

"No, not any more," I said. "It's all growing up to pine and blackberry bushes now. But anyway, just beyond that curve there's a road off to the side with a sign on a tree that says 'Saunders,' but you can't read it very well because the paint's all faded. Mr. Saunders used to own that land down there, but he sold it all to summer people two or three years ago. And a little ways along *that* road you come to another road that — "

"For John's sake!" the man spluttered. "*This* road and *that* road, and signs I can't read, and cows that aren't there! You've got me all mixed up. If I went down there in that wilderness, I'd be so lost that even the FBI couldn't find me. I'll just bet this is some stupid trick of Ziemer's. I suspected something right from the start. If he doesn't live here, why did he tell me to come to this house?"

Then it dawned on me. "You wouldn't be Dr. Kennedy?" I asked him.

"Sure I'm Kennedy. And a first-class fool, too, for listening to that practical joker."

"But he wasn't joking," I said. "We really do have a dinosaur. It just hatched out yesterday morning."

"How do you know it's a dinosaur? Who told you?"

"Dr. Ziemer did."

Dr. Kennedy scowled. "Just as I thought," he said. "What's the matter up here in New Hampshire? Don't people know that dinosaurs died out sixty million years ago?" He put his suitcase down on the porch floor. "Well, don't just stand there. Show me this animal of yours, whatever it is. I might as well look at it after coming all this way."

We had just started down the porch steps when a car stopped in front of the house. Dr. Ziemer got out. When he saw Dr. Kennedy he smiled and waved his hand.

"Hello, Kennedy. You made good time. How'd you get here so soon?"

"So soon? Good grief, I've been traveling all over New England trying to get to this place. I took a plane to Portsmouth, and a train from there to some place in the middle of nowhere, and then I got a ride on a bread truck to some other abandoned place and walked from there to here, and by golly, Ziemer, if this is another of your professional jokes, I swear I'll skin you and stuff you and put you in the museum on exhibit as a degenerate ape."

"All right, old man, just cool down," Dr. Ziemer said. "Just let us show you the dinosaur, and then you'll be convinced. After that you can have some breakfast and you'll feel better."

I led the way out to the chicken yard, and into Uncle Beazley's pen. The chickens were scratching around nearby, and they cocked their heads at us.

"There," Dr. Ziemer said. "Now maybe you'll believe me. Just bend down and look into that box there and see for yourself. Probably the only living dinosaur ever seen by man. One of the most remarkable happenings known to science."

Dr. Kennedy gave him a kind of dubious look, and then he bent way over. He was awfully tall, and he had a hard time getting his head down that far. He looked into the box.

Dr. Ziemer waited for a while for the sight to sink in, and then he said, "Well?"

"Well, what?" Dr. Kennedy said. "I don't see anything in here. Just an empty box."

"*What?*" we both said at once. We got down and looked in. Sure enough, it was empty.

"Good heavens!" the doctor said. "He's gotten out. Quick! We've got to find him." He ran around the pen, looking this way and that.

Dr. Kennedy slowly stood up straight and put his hands on his hips. He began to look pretty black. "Ziemer . . ." he said. "I suspected all along that you — "

"Oh cut it out, Kennedy," Dr. Ziemer said. "Can't you see we're not fooling? This is no joke, I tell you. Help us find this thing before he gets away. We just *can't* lose him. It would be a terrible loss to science."

I looked across the chicken coop, and just at that moment I happened to notice a chicken standing by the fence. She was tilting her head to one side the way hens do when they see something new. And then while I was watching, she slipped through the fence and started pecking at some grass outside. I went over and looked at the fence. There was a place where two sections met that had been pushed apart, and it left a space big enough for a chicken to get through.

I showed it to Dr. Ziemer.

"Hmmm, I see," he said. "He probably crawled under his own pen and pushed right through here. He wanted some grass, no doubt. We'll have to hunt for him in that long grass. You run into the house and get your sister to help us, and I'll start looking right away."

I dashed into the house. Cynthia was doing the breakfast dishes, and Mom was rolling out piecrust.

"Why Nate, where have you been?" Mom wanted to know.

"Dr. Kennedy's come," I said, "and we went out to show him the dinosaur, and he was gone — he must have slipped through the fence — and we're looking for him in the deep grass, and we've got to find him before he gets away — "

"Looking for Dr. Kennedy?" Mom said, kind of astonished. "Why, he only just got here, didn't he?"

"No, no, not for Dr. Kennedy — for Uncle Beazley — and it would be terrible if we couldn't find him."

Pop came in from the other room. "C'mon, Cynthia," he said, "let's go help."

We all streamed out of the house, and when I looked back, there was Mom coming too. She had the long-handled mop.

We all went back and forth through the grass patch, but no Uncle Beazley. Then we went into the goat's pasture and looked around there. The grass was pretty short in there, but we didn't see a sign of Uncle Beazley anywhere. I was poking along the fence in back of Mrs. Parsons's house, where she has some flower beds.

"Good morning, Nate," Mrs. Parsons said. "What are all you folks looking for out there anyway? And you've got

company too. I never saw such carryings-on. The goat get out?" She was cutting some flowers with a big pair of scissors.

"No, ma'am," I said. "It isn't the goat. She's right over there in the lot."

"Well, then, what is it? You don't have to be so mysterious about it, do you?"

"Well, the fact is, we've lost a little — er, a little animal."

"What kind of an animal? My gracious, you're being awfully close about it. Is it a cat?"

I figured I might as well tell her, but I wasn't sure how she would take it. "No, ma'am," I said, "it's not a cat. It's a small dinosaur."

Mrs. Parsons straightened up and gave me a funny look, and then she started to smile. "My land, Nate, how you talk! I didn't know you meant a *toy* animal. I thought you were looking for a *live* one. Why, hear the boy talk! I'm looking for a small dinosaur, he says."

While she was talking, I saw something move in among the gladioli. I kept my eye on it, and pretty soon a head stuck out. It was Uncle Beazley, all right, and he was chewing happily on a gladiola stalk as if it was the best thing he ever tasted. Mrs. Parsons hadn't noticed anything yet, and she was still going on talking.

"Ha, ha!" Mrs. Parsons laughed. "When you said you were looking for a small dinosaur, you gave me quite a turn for a moment because I thought you meant — oh! Mercy! What's *that?*"

I slipped over the fence in a flash and picked up Uncle Beazley. He was still chewing on the flower stalk just as if nothing had happened at all.

Mrs. Parsons backed off a ways and pointed her finger at Uncle Beazley. "Take it away!" she shouted. "Take it away this *minute!* He's eating my gladioli!"

I guess everyone heard all the racket. They came running across the field, and Dr. Ziemer was all smiles, he was so glad we'd found the dinosaur again, and Pop was apologizing to Mrs. Parsons.

She was pretty nice about it, and said that he'd only taken one of the gladioli, and that was a yellow one that she didn't care much for anyway. She'd always been interested in dinosaurs, she said. She used to read about them when she was a girl, but she hadn't supposed they ever came that small.

"That's a real little one you've got there," she said. "Kind of cute, isn't it?" But she didn't offer to come any nearer, I noticed.

Well, all this while Dr. Kennedy had been just standing

there with his mouth open staring at Uncle Beazley. Then he opened and shut his mouth a few times, but couldn't seem to say anything. Finally he grabbed Dr. Ziemer by the arm, pointed at the dinosaur, and said in a kind of strangling voice, "Great Scott, Ziemer, you were right! It is!" He turned as white as a sheet, and grabbed hold of the fence to steady himself.

Well, they finally got Mrs. Parsons quieted down, and Dr. Ziemer introduced Dr. Kennedy to everybody, and Pop introduced Dr. Ziemer to Mrs. Parsons, and after everything was all straightened out, we took Uncle Beazley back to his pen. We drove in some stakes to hold the wire down tight so he wouldn't get out again.

Mom went in to get some breakfast for Dr. Kennedy, and Dr. Ziemer began telling Dr. Kennedy all about the egg, and how large it was.

"Nate," he said all at once. "I think your dinosaur has grown. Surely he wasn't that big yesterday, was he?"

He got out the scales and his tape measure. I put Uncle Beazley on the scales, but he didn't seem to fit on them as well as before.

"Seven pounds!" Dr. Ziemer said. "Why, that's more than *twice* what he weighed yesterday. He's doubled his weight in twenty-four hours! Think of that, Kennedy."

"I am thinking of it. I wish I could say the same for myself. I'm just about starved. Do you suppose breakfast is ready?"

"Why, I'd forgotten all about that. Nate, why don't you take Kennedy in to breakfast? And see that he doesn't eat too many biscuits, even if you have to take a few yourself. I'll just finish these measurements while you're eating."

That sounded like a good idea to me. It was almost ten o'clock in the morning now, and I hadn't eaten a thing since breakfast.

Chapter Nine

AFTER BREAKFAST DR. KENNEDY AND DR.
Ziemer went out on the front porch to make plans. Dr. Ziemer
beckoned to me to come with them, but Dr. Kennedy didn't
pay any attention to me at all.

"I agree with you, of course, Ziemer," Dr. Kennedy said,
stretching out in the old wicker chair and crossing his long
legs. "We've got to release some sort of story to the press
about this remarkable animal. We could call the museum in
Washington and give them all the details, and they can pass
it on to the Associated Press and the other news services. Of
course the radio will pick it up right away, and it will be all
over the country in no time."

"And then the excitement begins," Dr. Ziemer said.

"Yes, exactly. Now, my point is this. I think we should have
this animal safely tucked away in the National Museum before we begin to spread the news. It's too valuable to take any

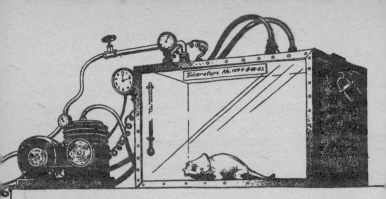

chances with it. Why, it's the most important living specimen in the whole *world*. We should put it in an air-conditioned, thermostatically controlled, constant-humidity glass compartment, and keep the animal away from drafts, germs, insects, crowds, and sudden changes of temperature. We wouldn't want to have crowds of people climbing all over us before we have a chance to crate the thing up and get it down to Washington. You know what a nuisance *that* can be."

That gave me a jolt. Were they going to take Uncle Beazley right off like that? I hadn't expected that to happen. But Dr. Ziemer looked over at me and winked.

"Hold on a minute, Kennedy," he said. "Have we asked the owner about this? Maybe he has other plans for his dinosaur."

"The owner? What do you mean?"

"Well, this dinosaur happens to belong to Nate Twitchell. Perhaps he doesn't want his dinosaur to go off to the museum. He may even want to keep it himself."

Kennedy sat up suddenly. "Well, he'll sell it, won't he?" He turned to me. "How about it, boy? We can give you a hundred dollars for your animal, right as it stands. You wouldn't want to turn down an offer like that, would you? How about it?"

A hundred dollars! That was an awful lot for one little dinosaur. But I'd only had him for one day now, and I didn't want to have him go off to a museum, and perhaps never have a chance to see him or anything. It just didn't seem right to sell him like that.

I shook my head. "No thanks," I said. "I don't think I better sell him."

"Well, a hundred and fifty dollars then. How about that?"

I shook my head again.

Dr. Kennedy sort of tightened up his mouth, and he turned to Dr. Ziemer. "What's the matter with the boy anyway? Are all New Hampshire people as stubborn as that?"

Dr. Ziemer smiled. "They're not stubborn, Kennedy. They just like to do things their own way. It is a very admirable quality."

Dr. Kennedy was frowning. "Now look here, boy. This is an important matter. This dinosaur is extremely valuable to science. We've never had anything like it, and we may never again. But what is it to you? It's just a big lizard. It wouldn't make a good pet. It would be hard to feed and take care of.

It couldn't stand cold weather. It would be just a nuisance to you. It wouldn't mean anything to a boy your age. Why don't you let us have it?"

"But he's mine," I said. "He's kind of a — well, kind of a friend. I wouldn't want to sell him."

Kennedy got up and began walking up and down the porch, waving his long arms. "But don't you see what it *means*? Scientists all over the world would give *anything* to be able to study this dinosaur. You wouldn't want to stand in the way of science, would you?"

"Well, no," I said. "But can't the scientists come here and study him? I don't mind if they *study* him, as long as I can keep him."

Dr. Ziemer grinned at me. "I guess you'd better give it up, Kennedy. The scientists will just have to come up here to Freedom, whether they like it or not."

"But good grief, Ziemer, where are they going to stay? There just aren't any accommodations here — no hotel, no restaurant, no inn. Do you expect them to camp out in the street?"

"Well, it's a nice quiet street," Dr. Ziemer said. "Besides, I don't recall hearing of any hotels in the Gobi Desert, or at the Wyoming fossil beds. Now, let's get that telegram off to the museum. Can I say that we agree that it appears to be a Triceratops?"

"Well, I suppose so," Kennedy said. I left them writing their telegram, and went out to get some more grass for Uncle Beazley. If he was going to grow that fast, I'd have to really get going on the grass supply.

Pretty early in the afternoon Cynthia got a telephone call from the Natural History Museum in New York. They wanted to know about the "dinosaur bones" that had been just discovered up in Freedom, New Hampshire. Dr. Ziemer straightened them out on that, and they said some men would come up right away to have a look. A few minutes later the *New York Herald Tribune* called about "the fossils," and then there was just a steady stream of calls from all over the place, and during supper a reporter from Laconia dropped in, and a college professor came over from his summer place on Sebago Lake. People were standing around asking all kinds of questions, and the telephone was ringing just about all the time, and then when we listened to the news on the radio, we heard a deep voice saying:

". . . And the strangest news tonight, folks, comes from the little village of Freedom, New Hampshire, where they claim a *dinosaur* has hatched out of a hen's egg, at the home of Mr. Walter Twitchell. Two scientists from the National Museum in Washington have examined the animal, and report that to the best of their knowledge it is a healthy specimen of Triceratops, a dinosaur that became extinct some sixty million years ago. So far the two scientists have offered no explanation for the fact that this ancient reptile has hatched from a hen's egg.

"Now, folks, when it comes to soap, the first thing we look for is — "

We turned off the radio and went back to answering the telephone. It sounded funny to hear our own name coming right over the radio, just as if it was some other family that we'd never heard of. After the news broadcast the telephone calls began coming thick and fast, and Cynthia really had her hands full. She was having fun, though, and I had to wipe dishes in her place, so I didn't pity her too much. There were calls from all over the place. There was one from Boothbay, and another from Prouts Neck, wherever that is, and then one came from a professor somebody over at Dartmouth College, and from the Animal Farm down in Nashua, and the Boston Museum of Science, and I don't know where all. It kept on all evening, and finally Pop told Mrs. Beebe, the telephone operator, that we were all going to bed, and not to ring our number any more until morning.

The next morning I did my chores as quick as I could. I almost forgot old Ezekiel down in the cellar, there was so much going on. I fed the chickens and milked the goat, and got a big armful of grass for Uncle Beazley. He looked even bigger than before, and his legs were getting stronger. I figured he'd be out of that pen again pretty soon if we didn't make it tighter.

We hadn't hardly started breakfast when the phone rang. It was a newsreel outfit down in Concord that wanted to come up and make some pictures. Then a television man made an appointment for the next day. Pop started in on a big article for the *Freedom Sentinel* about the dinosaur, and he had me write a piece on how it feels to own a dinosaur. Later he got Dr. Ziemer to write out some of the scientific things about it. Dinosaur news filled up about half the front page, and Pop ran off a lot of extra copies of the paper.

"Well," Pop said, "I guess the town of Freedom's back on the map again. It's the first time anybody's heard of us since back in 1932, when we had the eclipse up here. We'd better make the most of it while we can. Even a dinosaur won't make us famous for long. Nate, you better take about fifty copies of the paper over to the grocery store, and we can put some on a table in front of the house."

Pretty soon some of the neighbors began to drift in to look at the dinosaur. Mrs. Parsons looked at it and kind of shuddered. Joe Champigny's father just stared and shook his head. Mrs. Dunn brought her two children over to see the "funny animal," and then she went into the house to talk to Mom, and

I had to keep stopping them from throwing stones at Uncle Beazley. They're only little kids, but they sure can be a nuisance.

Dr. Ziemer and Dr. Kennedy came over, and right after that the newsreel truck drove up. The men got out a lot of equipment and cameras and stuff and dragged wires all over the place. They took pictures of the house, and had me pick up Uncle Beazley and feed him some grass, and I had to say something into a microphone about how I first saw him after he hatched out, and then Dr. Ziemer had to make a sort of speech about what kind of a dinosaur it was, and what a big thing this was for science and so on and so on. We all got pretty tired of being told to stand here and stand there and do this and do that. We were glad when the newsreel truck left.

And then came the reporters. There were an awful lot of them, and they kept coming in two or three at a time, and they took all kinds of pictures, and they all asked the same questions about how old I was and was I surprised to find a dinosaur come out of a hen's egg, and they talked all the time with cigarettes dangling out of the corner of their mouths. By that time there was getting to be quite a crowd, especially out in the back yard.

Dr. Ziemer and I stood right close to Uncle Beazley's pen so nobody would come along and hurt him. I don't know why it is, but whenever people see an animal in a cage or some place where they can reach him, they always want to poke him or throw things at him, or bother him in some way. I guess it must be a kind of instinct or something.

The scientists began arriving soon after that. There were all shapes and sizes of them. Some of them were tall and skinny and smoked big pipes, and others were short and had horn-rimmed glasses. They gathered in little circles and started jabbering away about "Mesozoic," and "Cretaceous," and "Protoceratops" and "atavism," and all sorts of words that were way over *my* head. And then the way they would *argue*. It was really something. Every one of them had a different theory, I guess, and each one was trying to talk louder and faster than the next man to prove that his theory was right and the others were all wrong. It made quite a racket, even worse than our sixth grade when Miss Watkins leaves the room.

Dr. Ziemer was busy shaking hands with old friends, and I could see Dr. Kennedy's head above the crowd. He was frowning and muttering things to himself like, "Place is a madhouse . . . bedlam . . . no order at all . . . completely unscientific . . . ought to be in a well-regulated museum . . . " and things like that.

I went to get another armful of grass, and I fed it to Uncle Beazley, and all the scientists crowded around and watched him eat, and of course they all had to argue about *that*. Some-

one said something about "mandibles," and they had to thrash that all out, and then there was a hot argument about "three-root molars," and it went on that way for the longest kind of a time. As far as I could see, Uncle Beazley was just *eating*, but they couldn't let it go at that. Scientists really sound pretty funny when you listen to them talk that way.

When evening came and it got dark, we sort of shooed everyone out so we could go in and have supper. It was pretty late, and Mom wasn't too pleased about having to keep supper so long for us.

"The idea," she said, "supper at almost eight o'clock. I don't see why everyone has to get in such a state over a little animal like that, even if it is a dinosaur. You'd think the world was coming to an end."

"But it's very important to the scientific world," I said.

"Oh, you and your scientific world," Mom said. "I should think the scientific world would know when it was time to go home for supper, instead of hanging around to all hours and making people late for their meals."

I don't think Mom ever *could* see what was so important about dinosaurs.

Chapter Ten

WELL, THE CROWDS KEPT GATHERING THAT way for almost a week, but after that it began to quiet down a little. The *Freedom Sentinel* had never sold so many copies before, and Pop had to run through a second printing of about two thousand copies to keep up with all the visitors. The grocery store ran out of ice cream and soft drinks every day except Thursday, when we had a thunderstorm in the middle of the afternoon.

By Saturday things had calmed down again. There were just one or two people at a time now, mostly scientists from way off somewhere like Wisconsin or Kentucky that couldn't get here any sooner. One very dignified-looking man with a big beard came all the way from Toronto, Canada. He stood looking at Uncle Beazley for the longest time. Finally he turned to Dr. Ziemer and said, "I say, I do believe you're right.

When I first heard the news I thought you American paleontologists had gone off half-cocked about this, but I must say, I have been quite convinced. Quite. Ah . . . you must be Kennedy, from the National Museum?"

"No, I'm Ziemer. And you're from Toronto, you said?"

"Yes, Morrison's the name."

Dr. Ziemer looked awfully pleased. "Why, Professor Morrison," he said, "I'm very happy to see you! It was very good of you to come. You know, I must admit I've had my doubts about whether this really *is* a dinosaur, but if you agree, then I'm not going to worry any more."

Professor Morrison smiled. "You know, Ziemer, I'm curious about what you plan to *do* with this amazing specimen. Will you be able to take good care of him? I'm never sure what you Americans may do with valuable things like this. You're all such superbusinessmen over here that I shouldn't be at all surprised if you sold this animal to Hollywood, or used it to advertise a frankfurter stand. You will be careful of it, won't you?"

"You'd better to speak to the owner," Dr. Ziemer said, pointing to me. "Nate Twitchell, this is Professor Albert Morrison, the world's greatest authority on dinosaurs."

"So you're the owner," Professor Morrison said, and his eyes sort of twinkled as he talked to me. "My boy, you have a *most* remarkable creature here. It's very precious to us all.

And it's precious because it's *alive* — remember that, won't you? I hope you'll do everything you can to *keep* it alive."

"Yes, sir," I said. "I will."

"Good boy," Professor Morrison said. "I know we can count on you."

Later that afternoon I sat down under the maple tree in the yard to see what the newspapers had to say about Uncle Beazley. I'd been so busy the last few days I hadn't had a chance. This is what the *New York Times* had said:

LIVE DINOSAUR HATCHES
FROM HEN'S EGG

FREEDOM, N. H., August 4
Scientists from all over the country
are flocking to the little town of Freedom to see their first living dinosaur,
which hatched recently from a hen's
egg on the farm of Nathan Twitchell.

Just how this animal, whose race
has been extinct for millions of years,
could have hatched from a hen's egg
is unexplained. Paleontologists have
gathered here from New York, Boston,
Philadelphia, Chicago, and elsewhere
over the United States, and they all
agree that it actually is a dinosaur,
of the type known as Triceratops, a
grass-eating reptile with three horns
and a great bony collar over its neck.
This species of dinosaur is known to
have reached the length of more than
twenty feet, weighing ten tons when
fully grown.

I heard someone walking up the path, so I put down the
paper. There was a man in a blue shirt, carrying his coat over
his arm.

"Hello, Mac," he said. "Is this the place with the dinosaur?"

"Yup," I said.

"Your name Nathan Twitchell?"

"Yup."

"Kin I look at the dinosaur?"

"Sure," I said, and led him out to Uncle Beazley's pen. Uncle Beazley was asleep, stretched out on his side in the sunshine.

"You sure he's alive?" the man said.

"Sure is. You see him breathing?"

The man nodded. "My name's Bill Griner. I got a gas station up to Conway, and I heard about this dinosaur you got down here. I got to thinking that would be a swell thing to have in a cage outside my gas station. The stations are all doing that now — they got bears, or a raccoon, or maybe a monkey. It's good for business. People stop and buy gas at a place that's got animals. Now if I had this dinosaur up there, I'd put up a big sign — 'Only living dinosaur in the world' — and just about *everybody* would stop to see it, and buy gas. See what I mean?"

I nodded. I saw what he meant, all right, but somehow I didn't take to the idea.

"Well now, how much do you want for him?" the man said. "I'd be willing to give you a good price."

"Oh, no, thanks," I said. "I want to keep him."

"But look, kid, I'm offering you real money. You got no use

for a dinosaur, and you got all that work taking care of him and feeding him an' all that. Just let me take him off your hands and you can make a nice profit on him. Whatta you say?"

"I just don't want to sell him," I said.

"But what's the sense of that, kid? What *good* is it to you? It's too ugly for a pet. And there's no market for dinosaurs these days. And it's going to be a big expense to feed in the winter."

"But I said I wanted to keep him," I told the man.

"But I don't see it," he said, looking kind of annoyed at me. "You're not using it for anything and I could make good money on it. Why don't you let me have it?"

"But I just want to keep it," I said. "Isn't that all right if I just want to have it? Do I have to have a reason for everything?"

The man shrugged his shoulders and turned away. "Well, okay, kid, have it your own way. But if you change your mind let me know. Here's my address." He gave me a slip of paper and walked back to his red pickup truck. He raced the engine a few times, and spun the truck around and zoomed off up the street, leaving a big cloud of dust behind.

Almost every day there'd be somebody who wanted me to sell Uncle Beazley to him for some reason or other. A great big yellow convertible drove up one time, and a smooth-looking man with a little bit of black mustache got out. He started to offer me a cigarette from a silver cigarette case, but then he changed his mind, I guess.

"Does Mr. Nathan Twitchell live here?" he asked.

I told him yes.

"Is he home?"

"Yup."

"Well, run along and tell him I'd like to speak with him on business."

He turned away and didn't pay any more attention to me, as if he was a king or something and I was just there to run errands for him. I didn't like his highhanded manner too much, so I just stood there. Pretty soon he turned around and frowned at me.

"Didn't I tell you I wanted to speak with Mr. Nathan Twitchell?" he said. "Don't waste my time, young man."

"You are speaking to him," I said. "I'm Nate Twitchell."

He changed his manner then.

"Oh — " he said. "I — I understand you're the owner of a live dinosaur. Well, I'm the vice-president of the Old Mill Pond Whiskey Corporation. I have a little proposition for you. I'd like to rent your dinosaur for a while, so we can use it in our big advertising campaign."

I couldn't see what a dinosaur had to do with whiskey. So I finally asked him about it.

"Why, it's perfectly obvious," he said. "What's the most important thing about any whiskey?"

I wasn't too sure about that, not having had any. "The way it tastes?" I said.

"Not at all," he said. "No two people could ever agree about how any drink tastes. That's just a matter of personal opinion. The most important thing about a whiskey is how *old* it is. Then you can talk about facts, you see. Whiskey A is two years old, and Whiskey B is three years old — so everybody buys Whiskey B. It's as simple as that."

"How old is Old Mill Pond?" I asked him.

He lowered his voice a little. "Well, just between you and me, it isn't any too old. That's why we need some really hot advertising. That's where the dinosaur comes in."

"But how can the dinosaur make it any older?" I said.

"It doesn't actually *make* it any older. It makes it *seem* older. That's the whole secret of advertising, my boy. And that's why the distillers always have pictures of old mills and rocking chairs and grandfathers on their labels. Now what could be older than a dinosaur? You just can't beat it. It's the oldest thing around. If the idea catches on we might even change the name of our brand to Old Dinosaur, or Old Fossil — er, no, that sounds too dry. Perhaps Old Jurassic. We'll be the oldest-sounding drink on the market, and we'll make a fortune."

"But what would you do with the dinosaur?" I asked.

"Oh, we'd put him on display in a big truck, and paint it all up in flashy colors, and put banners on the top, hire a sound truck and tour the country. It'll make Old Mill Pond the best-known name in the business. It would be a wonderful thing for us."

"I don't think it would be a wonderful thing for the dinosaur," I said. "All that racket and moving around would probably make him sick."

"Don't worry about that," the man said. "We'd pay you two hundred dollars a month while he lived. He'd last long enough to make good money out of him."

I thought about that two hundred dollars a month. But finally I shook my head. "I don't guess I better."

The man threw up his hands. "But what *are* you going to do with him, then?"

"I'm not going to *do* anything with him," I said. "I just want to have him. Isn't it enough just to *have* something?"

"Not when you can make money on it," the man said. He took a printed card out of a case and gave it to me. "Now when you get tired of just *having* this dinosaur, let me know, will you?" He walked back to his big yellow car and drove away.

I think it was just a few days later that a letter came from the McDermis Luggage Company.

We were interested to hear that you have come into possession of a live dinosaur. As you may know, we are manufac-
turers of fine hand luggage, and make a specialty of luggage
in a wide variety of unusual leathers, such as buffalo calf,
gemsbok, baby whale and iguana. It occurred to us that you
might be willing to let us have your dinosaur for this pur-
pose. We assure you that we are prepared to make you a
very good offer, for there is no other dinosaur hide on the
market at present.

Sincerely,
Edward P. McDermis
President

I didn't like *that* idea very much. Imagine making Uncle
Beazley into a suitcase! It made me shiver just to think of it.

Well, things went on this way for a week or so, with people
coming in every now and then, perhaps only about twenty
people a day. Some of them had some pretty queer ideas. One
man came with one of those tape recorder things, and he said
he wanted to record "the voice of prehistoric time." He spent
most of the afternoon trying to get Uncle Beazley to make
some sort of noise. The man squeaked and growled and
barked and roared at him. Then the man finally got dis-
gusted, and said some things to himself that I bet he wouldn't
want to have recorded. Then he went away.

The dinosaur had been growing like anything, and by the
middle of August he was a good five and a half feet long,

counting his tail, and about two and a half feet high. He'd
gotten too heavy for the kitchen scales when he was five days
old, and after that we had to get two bathroom scales and lay
a plank over them, and then get Uncle Beazley to stand on the
plank. We'd read what the two scales said, and add them together, and then subtract what the plank weighed. Dr. Ziemer's notebook went along like this:

August 12	length, 5′1″	weight, 106 lbs
August 13	" 5′3½″	" 121 "
August 14	" 5′6″	" 144 "

You can see that he was really coming right along. The
doctor was the most surprised man. He said he'd never
known any animal to grow *that* fast. He used to stand
there and puzzle over it while he was watching Uncle Beazley eat.

"I know reptiles can grow very fast," he told me. "Take alligators, for instance. They can grow to be six feet long in five years, and then when they're big enough to take care of themselves, they slow down. But this fellow has grown to almost six feet in *two weeks*. Of course the Triceratops was living in an age of big animals, and I suppose they had to grow fast in order to survive, but still . . . this is an unbelievable rate of growth. I wonder . . . perhaps the quality of the modern atmosphere is different from what it was sixty million years ago. Perhaps his metabolism has been speeded up . . . That's just a guess, of course. But anyway, Nate, if he goes along at this rate much longer, we're going to have a *problem* on our hands."

Getting food for the dinosaur was a problem already. I ran out of grass around our place in just a few days. Then I used to go down to the old Spencer place at the end of the street. The grass is just growing wild there, around the house and in the back lot. Joe Champigny would go along with me, and we'd take my old express wagon with the sides on it. We'd take turns with the scythe, and when we'd cut enough for one day, we'd pile it all on the wagon and tie it on with a clothesline and pull it back to my house. It was hot work, but it was worth it to see old Uncle Beazley plow into a pile of green grass. He just loved to eat.

That was all right for a while, but then we found we had to begin making two trips a day because one load wasn't enough. Joe was beginning to complain that he wasn't getting any time to go fishing any more, and it wouldn't be long before we'd be out of grass at the Spencer place. Pop suggested that we get old Henry Smith to cut us a patch of grass every couple of days with his tractor. Henry Smith mows the sides of the town roads, and so he has his mowing machine out most of the time. That worked pretty well. Dr. Ziemer borrowed a trailer from the garage, and we could haul a big pile of grass and dump it in our back yard, and that would last for two or three days.

Of course, by this time the dinosaur was much too big to keep in that little pen. We had to give that up when he was about a week old. We decided that the only thing to do was to tether him, so we got a strong leather collar and a cow chain, and drove a big crowbar into the ground and fastened the chain to that. It worked pretty well, and Uncle Beazley didn't seem to mind it at all. He was very friendly with me, and never tried to bite or poke at me with his horns. He was kind of nervous with other people, though, and he didn't like loud noises. They seemed to make him angry.

Dr. Ziemer told me I ought to exercise Uncle Beazley every day, since he was tied up that way, so I would take him for a walk in the mornings. I used to do it before breakfast, when it was quiet and cool, and we'd walk up the street to the school and back. It felt pretty queer walking along with that strange animal shuffling along behind me, his head slowly wagging back and forth, and his big tail dragging in the dust.

Chapter Eleven

WELL, UNCLE BEAZLEY KEPT ON GROWING. According to Dr. Ziemer's notebook, he was six feet nine inches long and weighed three hundred and sixty pounds by the twentieth of August, and at the end of the month he was an even nine feet and weighed seven hundred and ninety-eight pounds. He was so heavy now that we had to give up the two bathroom scales and instead we used the old hay scales down in front of Beeman's feed store. When we walked Uncle Beazley down there every day, people would come out on their front porches and watch us go by, and all the kids in town would follow along behind. They didn't come any too close, though. Uncle Beazley's horns had begun to grow, and he looked something like an armored tank with guns sticking out the front end.

Mr. Beeman, who runs the feed store, always came out on the platform to watch the weighing.

"Morning, Doctor," he said. "Hello there, Nate. What's the reading this morning?"

I slid the balance weights along the bar until it balanced. "Eight-nine-seven," I called to him, while Dr. Ziemer wrote it down in his notebook. That was the second of September, I remember.

"What you gonna do come winter, Nate?" Mr. Beeman wanted to know. "That animal of yours is goin' to use up a power of hay when the grass gives out. Have you got a shed for him, or can he stay out in cold weather?"

"Don't know," I said. "I never had a dinosaur before."

Dr. Ziemer didn't say anything just then, but later on that day the doctor had a talk with me.

"Nate," he said, "when does your cold weather begin up here?"

"Oh, the first frost comes about the middle of September. Why?"

He looked pretty serious about something. "Well, there's something you ought to know," he said. "You see, dinosaurs are reptiles, and they're not built for very cold weather. You know what turtles do in the winter, don't you?"

"Sure," I told him. "They go down to the bottom of the pond and dig into the mud and just lie there all winter."

"Right," said the doctor. "They don't eat, and scarcely breathe at all. You see, reptiles are cold-blooded animals. That means they don't have any way of heating themselves. When cold weather comes, reptiles just get cold, and they slow down to a stop. Some of them can't live in a cold climate.

"It may have been the cold weather at the end of the Cretaceous period that killed off the dinosaurs. Dinosaurs lived in a hot climate, and although Triceratops was the last of the horned dinosaurs, I doubt if even he could stand a New Hampshire winter."

Well, I'd expected this right along, but I kept putting it off, the way you do when the end of summer comes along, and you know that you've got to go back to school pretty soon, but you keep putting it out of your mind because it's so dismal to think about. I had a hunch that Uncle Beazley wasn't made for winter, since he didn't have any fur or anything. But I hadn't said anything about it, because it looked as if it would come to just one thing — that I wouldn't be able to keep my big old dinosaur much longer.

Dr. Ziemer looked at me for a while, and then he went on. "About the only thing to do," he said, "is to keep him indoors during the winter in a clean, warm, well-ventilated place. And I don't think your mother's going to want him in the parlor all winter."

"No. I guess not," I said, feeling pretty glum.

"And then there's the matter of feed," Dr. Ziemer went on. "We've used up just about all the available grass in the neighborhood, and when that's gone we'll have to start buying feed for him. He doesn't like hay. We've tried that. So it's going to be expensive during the winter, trying to satisfy a dinosaur's appetite."

"Well, what can we do?" I said, knowing pretty well what he would say.

"The only thing I can suggest is to ship him to a zoo, or a museum, where he can get proper housing and food. This whole thing has been a lot of care right from the start, and you've worked hard at it, and you've made a real pet out of this dinosaur, but the situation is getting too big for you to handle by yourself. We're just going to have to ask other people to help us. But it's going to be hard to give him up, though, isn't it, Nate?"

I had to swallow a couple of times. "Yeah," I said. I turned away and started kicking against the trunk of the maple tree. My eyes felt sort of funny, but I didn't want the doctor to think I was crying or anything like that. He stood there for a while, rubbing his chin with his hand.

"I tell you, Nate," he said. "Why don't you go over to the lake and see if you can hook a few fish for supper? Take Joe Champigny along with you, why not? I've got a few things to attend to this afternoon, and when you come back we can talk this over again. Oh — er, is your father over at the shop?"

"Yes, he is," I said, and went across the street to get Joe. We got our rods and the bait can and started down to the lake. When we got to the boat I put in the two sash weights I use for an anchor and then we pushed off. We rowed out to the middle of the lake, and then Joe slid the anchor into the water. It went down out of sight, and then some bubbles came up after it touched bottom.

We baited up and dropped in our lines, and then settled back with our feet up on the gunwales. It was one of those kind of slow, quiet days that come at the end of the summer, when everything feels sort of still and peaceful. You could see a little touch of red here and there along the shore where

a maple was beginning to turn, and a couple of crows were calling over on the far shore. You could hear the sounds coming over the water.

Joe felt a nibble and pulled up his line. The worm was gone as usual. Those sunfish are too smart. He baited up again, and threw in his line. The ripples went sliding out in big circles.

"What's the matter, Nate?" Joe said. "You look kind of sour."

"I've got to send my dinosaur away to some museum," I said. "They can't stay out when cold weather comes."

"Gee, that's tough. Can't you keep it in a shed some place? You could use the Simmonses' old carriage house."

"Too cold," I said. "Dinosaurs are cold-blooded. They've got to have a heated place. That's what Dr. Ziemer says."

"Aw, you could try it anyways. Why not?"

I shook my head. "I better not. It might die, and then how would I feel? I promised Professor Morrison that I would do everything I could to keep it alive. I guess I'll just have to give it up."

"Too bad, Nate," Joe said.

"Well, maybe sometime I can go to the museum and see Uncle Beazley again. He'd probably forget me though."

We had fairly good luck, and by the time the sun began to get low over the trees, Joe had three middle-sized bass, and I had two perch and a nice bass, about a pound and a half, I should say. We tied up the boat and walked back to town.

Dr. Ziemer was going to stay for supper, Mom said. She told me to get busy and clean the fish, and we could have them for supper. I got a bucket of water and sat on the back steps to clean the fish. Cynthia came out to peel some potatoes.

"I know something you don't know," Cynthia said in a low voice.

"All right, Sis," I said. "What is it? Blueberry pie for supper?"

"Nope," she whispered. "Nothing to eat. It's something about *you*. I heard Dr. Ziemer talking to Mom and Pop about it this afternoon."

"Well, what is it?"

"Can't tell," she said, and started peeling another potato.

"How about a hint, then? Just a *little* one? Come *on*, Sis."

"Well it's about you and — "

"*Cynthia!*" Mom called out. "Don't give away any secrets, now. Remember what we told you."

"I wasn't, Mom. I was just making Nate curious. I wasn't going to tell him anything. *Honestly*, I wasn't."

"Well, all right," Mom said. "Hurry up with those potatoes, now. Let's have those fish, Nate, and don't forget to feed the chickens. Cynthia, you run out and pick me about a quart of wax beans, will you? The ones down at the far end of the row are the biggest."

Supper was finally ready, and we all sat down and watched while Pop served out the bass. It was mighty good, and just about enough to go round, and then there were the perch to fill in the corners with. And we had boiled potatoes with melted butter running all over them, with a little parsley on top, and the wax beans had that real fresh taste to them, and

Mom had made corn muffins. I just stuffed myself till I was about bursting.

Finally I had a little more time to look around, and I noticed that everybody was sort of exchanging glances across the table. Dr. Ziemer raised his eyebrows and looked at Pop, and Pop nodded back at him.

"Ahem!" the doctor said, and wiped his mouth with his napkin. "Nate, if you can interrupt your eating for a few moments, I have a little proposition to put to you."

Here it comes, I thought. He's going to offer to take my dinosaur away with him.

"You remember, Nate, that we talked this morning about taking care of the dinosaur over the winter, and you agreed that there wasn't any place here that would be suitable. Now I have a suggestion, and I'd like to see what you think of it. If you are willing, we could ship the animal to Washington, and we could keep it at the National Museum. You could still be the owner, but the museum would provide the feed and the living quarters. What would you think of that?"

I suppose that was nice of the museum to offer to do that. It was pretty generous of them to keep Uncle Beazley for me and feed him and take care of him, but it still meant we would be a long way apart, and I'd probably *never* get a chance to see him way down there in Washington. I guess I didn't look any too enthusiastic about the idea, but when I looked up at

Dr. Ziemer his eyes were twinkling, and the corners of his mouth were twitching a little.

"And of course," Dr. Ziemer went on, very calmly, "it is understood that you would come along too, because we need your help in handling the — "

"*What?*" I shouted. "You mean I can go *too?* Oh, *boy!*" But then I remembered there was more to it than that. I looked at Mom and Pop, to see whether there was any *chance* that they might let me go. I was pretty sure there wasn't much hope for that, of course, but it wouldn't hurt to ask.

"Could I, Mom?" I said. "It would be awfully good experience for me. Couldn't I go? You heard what the doctor said. He said they needed me to take care of Uncle Beazley."

"Well, what do you think, Walt?" Mom said. She didn't sound as flustered as I expected. In fact, neither of them looked very surprised at the idea. I wondered if they'd talked it all over ahead of time. That must have been what Cynthia was talking about.

"I guess Nate's old enough to take care of himself for a while. I think perhaps we can manage around here fairly well without him. Of course he has been doing a lot of chores around the place. I think we could get Joe Champigny to take care of your chores, Nate, like the stovewood and the chickens."

"But that would cost money, wouldn't it, Pop?" I would

have been glad to pay Joe myself, if I had enough money. But I didn't.

"You could pay Joe out of your salary, Nate," Dr. Ziemer said.

"But I don't have a salary," I said.

"You will have. The museum will pay you twenty-five dollars a week for your services, and you can pay Joe out of that."

"Gosh!" I said. "That would be wonderful. When do we go?"

Dr. Ziemer rubbed his chin. "Well, the museum needs a little time to get ready for a dinosaur, and we've got to arrange for one of our trucks. I should say we wouldn't be able to leave for almost a week."

"Oh," I said. "But school begins the ninth of September. That wouldn't give me very much time at the museum, would it? Only a day or so. But, that's better than nothing, of course." Naturally I didn't want them to get the idea that I didn't want to *go* or anything like that. It just did seem too bad that school was going to begin so soon after I got down there.

"Oh, by the way, Nate," Pop said, as if he just happened to remember something. "I was speaking to Mr. Jenkins, your school principal, today, and he said that if you needed to take any trips during school time to help look out for your dinosaur, he could excuse you from attendance for . . . well . . . I think it was four weeks he said. He felt that there was so much you could learn from the experience that it would be worth the time lost from school."

"*Really?*" I said. "Good for Mr. Jenkins! I didn't think he had it in him."

"Well, it wasn't entirely his own idea," Pop said, with a look at Mom, "and he made a rather strong suggestion that you keep up in your schoolwork while you're away."

"Oh, I will," I said. "I'll work *twice* as hard as usual."

"I'll wager you could, too, without straining yourself," Mom said. Cynthia snickered, but I felt too good to kick her under the table the way I usually do.

"If you're studying science," Dr. Ziemer said, "we have some men at the museum who will be able to help you a little. And you can learn a lot wandering around in the museum. The Smithsonian Institution is just across the Mall from us, and so is the Arts and Industries Museum, and the National Art Gallery is just a block down the street. Then of course there's the Library of Congress, and the Capitol, and the Supreme Court, and if you like astronomy, there's the Naval Observatory. I think we can see that your education is not forgotten completely."

"Gee," I said, "you mean it's all worked out so I can go

down to Washington for a whole *month*, and I'll get paid for it, and I can even skip *school*? Boy, am I lucky! I must be dreaming or something."

I felt so good that I never even noticed what we had for dessert. And that doesn't happen very often.

Chapter Twelve

We LEFT FOR WASHINGTON ON THE MORN-
ing of the sixth of September. The truck had come the day
before, and we put in a good lot of straw for bedding, and a
trailer load of grass for food. It was high time we were leaving, because the town of Freedom was just about out of grass.
We'd used up all the grass for a couple of miles around, I
guess.

The nights had been cool lately, and Uncle Beazley was
kind of sluggish until he got warmed up. The morning we left
was gray and misty, and we could barely get the big dinosaur

to stand up and follow me to the truck. He was really sizable now. Dr. Ziemer's notebook for that day said ten feet, six inches (but it was hard to measure him exactly, his tail was so big), and his weight was eleven hundred and forty pounds. We had some big planks resting on the tail gate of the truck for a kind of ramp, but we couldn't get Uncle Beazley to walk up it. He just stood in back of the truck, wagging his big head slowly back and forth. I stood inside the truck and pulled on his chain, and Dr. Ziemer and Pop and the truck driver sort of pushed from behind, but it was no good. He didn't budge.

Finally I had an idea. I went over to Mrs. Parson's garden and picked a gladiola, and brought that back to the truck. Then I showed it to Uncle Beazley, and held it in front of his nose to smell. That sort of woke him up, I guess, and he lifted up his head and lumbered up the ramp into the truck, with his eye on the gladiola. The truck's springs sagged as he got in. As soon as he was all the way in, I gave him the gladiola and slipped out the back of the truck. Then we closed up the tail gate and fastened it.

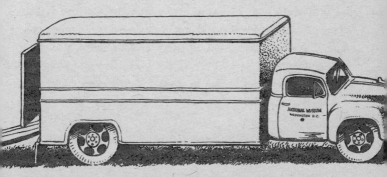

Mom and Pop and Cynthia were standing around to see us off, and Mom was asking if I had my extra pair of pajamas, and Pop was telling me to write some letters home. Dr. Ziemer was saying thank you and good-by to everybody, and the truck driver was reminding us that we'd better get going if we wanted to get to Washington before Christmas. I put my suitcase in Dr. Ziemer's car, and then climbed into the cab of the truck. I was supposed to see that Uncle Beazley didn't get too excited by all the noise. Just what I was going to do about it I didn't know, but at least he could see me through the little window and would know that I was going with him.

Finally the truck engine started, and after it was warmed up we pulled out into the street. I waved out the cab window, and as the truck rolled up the street I could see Mom and Pop and Cynthia waving from in front of the house, and then pretty soon I couldn't see them any more, and then the trees shut out the view and I couldn't even see the house. It was the first time I'd ever gone off and left the family like that, but I was too excited to think about that very much.

It was about half-past six in the morning when we started, and everything was all misty as we went by Ossipee Lake. When I looked back, I could just make out Dr. Ziemer's car coming along behind us. The truck driver's name was Michael Finney, and he told me all the places I ought to go to see in Washington, like the Washington Monument and the zoo. He'd been working for the National Museum for twenty years, he said, and he'd gone out years ago with an expedition to Wyoming to collect fossils.

"That was the Como Bluff dinosaur graveyard," he explained. "It's just out of Medicine Bow, Wyoming, and surely that's the loneliest, scariest country I've ever laid eyes on. It was the barest, forsakenest kind of a place, and all these big old bones coming out of the ground. I can tell you I was glad when that trip was over. If you want my personal opinion, I don't go for all these bones and things like that. Give me the live animal every time, and leave all the old bones lie. That's my view of the matter."

Later on the sun came out and the mist burned away, and it was as nice a September day as anybody could want. The hayfields along the road looked kind of clean and dry and pleasant, the way they do usually in the fall, and we didn't see hardly any cars on the road at that hour of the morning.

The first traffic we came to was down in Manchester. Just as we were coming into the city a man in a big shiny car tried to go past us, and he blew his horn right beside the truck. That must have startled Uncle Beazley, because I heard him heave around back there and bang his horn against the sides. I looked back through the window and spoke to him, but it was quite a while before he calmed down. He didn't like automobile horns for some reason, and all the rest of the trip I had to keep soothing him when he heard them blowing too near him.

It was an awful long ride. Michael Finney kept calling out the names of the cities as we went through them, so I could see where we were on the map. I could follow our route through Worcester, Massachusetts, and Hartford, Connecticut, and I remember going through New York all right, because horns were blowing just about all the time there, and I had to keep talking and talking to Uncle Beazley to keep him from banging around too much.

After New York, though, it got kind of confusing, and I couldn't tell where one city left off and the next one began. I never saw such a lot of houses and chimneys and factories and things. It looked as if the whole place was one big city, with gray smoke rising up all over the place and smudging up the sky so you could hardly tell whether it was a clear day or not. It was pretty late in the afternoon when we went past Philadelphia, and then we stopped somewhere and had supper at a place where you could put a nickel in a little box at the table, and some music would start playing somewhere else. Michael Finney showed me how to do it. You could pick out the music you wanted by punching a red button under the title. I picked one called "Night on the Pampas," because it was the only one that didn't sound mushy, but the music was pretty screechy. Dr. Ziemer said slot machine music was one of the great advantages of modern civilization, but I'm pretty sure he was kidding.

It was dark by the time we got back on the road again, and lights were flashing past all the time, and before long I must have fallen asleep, because the next thing I heard was Dr. Ziemer's voice saying, "All right, Mike, back her up to the rear entrance." I sat up and looked out. We were right beside a big dark building. When the truck stopped I got out and went around to the tail gate.

"Hello there, Nate," Dr. Ziemer said. "Welcome to Washington. I'm afraid we've kept you up very late."

"Don't you worry about him, Doctor," Michael Finney said. "He's been sound asleep all the way from Wilmington." He opened up the rear doors of the truck and we let down the tail gate. Dr. Ziemer pulled open a big door into the building, and turned on a light so we could see what we were doing. The loading platform was just as high as the floor of the truck, so we didn't have to use a ramp. This was a lucky thing, because Uncle Beazley was too long to turn around in the truck, and it was a tough job getting him to back up. Michael Finney sort of held up the tail to keep him pointed right, and the doctor and I took hold of the horns and pushed him backwards. I kept on talking to Uncle Beazley all the time so he wouldn't get excited or anything. He didn't want to budge at first, but finally he seemed to get the idea, and he backed out of the truck one step at a time. Then we swung him around and led him into the building.

We went down a long corridor, and almost ran down Dr. Kennedy, who came around a corner right in front of us. He gulped and squeezed back against the wall to let Uncle Beazley go by.

"My Lord!" Dr. Kennedy said. "He's as big as a horse! Isn't it dangerous to walk around with him that way? I don't like the looks of those horns."

"Don't worry," Dr. Ziemer said. "Nate knows how to handle him."

We led the dinosaur into a good-sized room at the end of the hall. There was a lot of straw on the floor, and it had a window with bars in it, and a good strong gate across the doorway.

"I got your grass finally," Dr. Kennedy said, pointing to a big pile of it in one corner. "It was an awful job. We had to send way out towards Gaithersburg to get it. It all came in fresh this morning, and there's half a ton of it there."

"Good. Fine," Dr. Ziemer said. "I guess everything's all set here. Now, I'll just speak to the night watchman about this, and then, Nate, we'll go over to my apartment and tumble into bed."

We said good night to Dr. Kennedy and to Michael Finney,

and then Dr. Ziemer and I walked around the corner of the museum.

He pointed out across the big open space. There was a big, tall, pointed pillar sticking straight up in the air, all white against the sky. It looked really beautiful, it was so clean and sharp-looking.

"That's the Washington Monument, Nate," Dr. Ziemer said. Then he pointed in the opposite direction. "And there's the Capitol."

I looked where he was pointing, and saw a long building with a great big dome on it, and the whole building was all lit up with bright lights. It was one of the grandest-looking buildings I ever saw. I don't think I'll ever forget that sight.

"Come on, Nate," the doctor said, pulling my arm a little. "We've got to get some sleep. We'll have plenty of time to see the sights in the next few weeks."

Chapter Thirteen

D<small>R. ZIEMER'S APARTMENT WAS ON TWELFTH</small> Street, just half a mile or so from the museum. At first it seemed very strange to hear all the cars going past the window all night long. I guess in a city there's always somebody awake, no matter how late it is. You don't notice the noise in the daytime, but when you lie in bed in the dark all those traffic sounds come in the window, and the glow of the lights goes back and forth on the ceiling. It used to keep me awake at first, but after a while I got used to it.

My first job every day was to take Uncle Beazley for a walk. Now that we were keeping him shut up in a room in the museum, Dr. Ziemer said it was specially important to see that he got some exercise and fresh air every day. We could do that outdoors until cold weather came, and then we'd have to exercise him indoors after that. But of course it wouldn't do to stroll around the city streets with that dinosaur in the daytime. Dr. Ziemer said the people in Washington weren't too accustomed to a live dinosaur and there might be all kinds of crowds and confusion, and we might get into trouble with the police. Besides, Dr. Kennedy wanted to keep Uncle Beazley out of sight as much as we could. He didn't want a whole lot of people piling into the museum and getting in the way.

"The way I look at it," Dr. Kennedy kept saying, "is that we've got to protect this animal from the public. If the public gets to know we've got a live dinosaur here, they'd be swarming all over the place, endangering his health and getting in our way all the time. And the public wouldn't have any scientific interest in the dinosaur. They would just come and gawk at him. That's why I haven't told the newspapers what we've got here. We might as well keep this thing quiet until we've had a chance to study the dinosaur for a while. I haven't even told the police about it yet."

Well, we decided that the best time to exercise Uncle Beazley was early in the morning, before people were out on the streets. So every morning I would get out of bed at about five o'clock, while it was still pretty dark outside. Then I'd get dressed and eat some breakfast, and walk over to the museum. It's pretty nice in a city early in the morning like that, when there's hardly anybody around and the streets are all quiet and empty. I would walk down Twelfth Street, and across

Pennsylvania Avenue, and then across Constitution Avenue, and there I'd be at the National Museum.

I would go in the back door, and tell the night watchman that I was going to take the dinosaur out, and he would hold the door open for us as we went out. He used to stand behind the door, too, because he never did like to get too close to Uncle Beazley.

"I don't see how you dare go around with that big fellow," he told me. "He could make mincemeat out of you in no time."

"Oh, he's pretty tame," I said. "He wouldn't hurt anything unless he got excited. He knows me pretty well. You see, I've taken care of him ever since he was hatched."

We'd usually walk for half an hour or so on the Mall, which is what they call that big open space with all the grass in between the Capitol and the Washington Monument. Usually there wouldn't be anybody else there, except perhaps a man way off walking his dog down near the General Grant statue, or now and then a milk truck going by. When we'd been out long enough, I'd take Uncle Beazley back into the museum, and have him all safely back in his room before most people were out in the streets.

When Dr. Ziemer arrived at the museum in the morning, he would give me some scientific thing to find out about, like the life cycle of the butterfly, or the formation of coal, or how

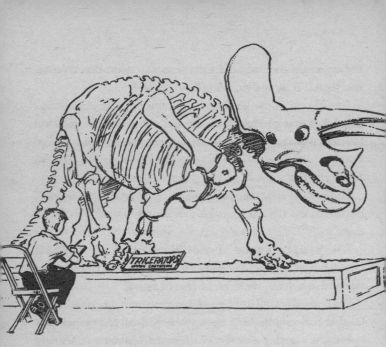

the glaciers covered North America, and then I would hunt around in the museum and find an exhibit about it, and study it pretty carefully, or perhaps draw a picture of it. Then I would go back to Dr. Ziemer and tell him what I found out. After that I would go to the office of the museum superintendent, and he would give me some of the museum accounts to figure out, and when I had done some of them, the secretary used to let me work them out on the adding machine to see if my answers were right. I really learned a lot in the museum, and it was more fun than school.

Sometimes when Dr. Ziemer had some free time he would take me to places like the Archives Building or the Supreme Court, and after I got to know my way around a little, I went to a lot of places by myself. The place I liked best was the Jefferson Memorial. It's a big round building, right beside a kind of a bay they call the Tidal Basin, and it's all made of white marble. I think they said the marble came from Vermont, but I liked it anyway. Inside, there's a statue of Thomas Jefferson, and one of his sayings is carved around the inside of the dome. I can't remember the exact words, but the general idea was that he didn't think much of making up other people's minds for them. Dr. Ziemer said he liked that building best too.

Well, things went along like that for about two weeks, and Uncle Beazley was growing all that time. We tried out different kinds of feed on him, because it was too hard to get fresh grass, and we finally decided on alfalfa, with about fifty pounds of poultry mash for dessert. He used to eat up about four bags of alfalfa a day, along with about ten gallons of water. I never saw such an appetite. By September twenty-fifth he measured sixteen feet and weighed two thousand, six hundred and seventy-four pounds. His upper horns were almost as long as my arm, and the lower horn on his nose was about half as long. His head was about three feet long, and the bone collar had grown up over his neck and shoulders.

He was terribly strong. We had given up using the leather collar and the cow chain, because we couldn't find a collar big enough for his neck, and besides, he could easily break the chain if he wanted to. Instead of that, I used to tie a piece of rope around his left upper horn and lead him that way. If he ever had really wanted to go somewhere else when I was leading him, I couldn't have done a thing about it. Dr. Ziemer said that dinosaurs had very small brains and weren't very bright, but Uncle Beazley knew me and trusted me, and so he would follow me around. That was a lucky thing, because I sure couldn't pull him.

In the early mornings, sometimes, when there was nobody else around, I would climb up on Uncle Beazley's back and have a ride. The easiest way to get up was to put my left foot on the base of one of the big horns, grab hold of his bone collar, and swing up on his back. It was kind of a slope forward, but his skin was pretty rough, like coarse sandpaper, and that kept me from sliding too much. I could steer him by pulling left or right on the rope. He didn't move very fast, so there wasn't much danger of running into things.

Then one morning a dreadful thing happened. I think it was almost the end of the month, and I'd taken Uncle Beazley out as usual for his morning exercise. It was very misty close to the ground, but higher up the air was clear, and I could see the top of the Washington Monument high up in the air. I climbed up on Uncle Beazley, and he started walking along slowly. I headed him toward the Washington Monument. It was kind of fun on a morning like this, because all the big buildings on each side of the Mall, like the Interstate Commerce Building and the Department of Agriculture, fade away into the mist and look like gray cliffs and rocks, and I could imagine I was a prehistoric man riding around and discovering new places and things. It was pretty exciting, but not anywhere near as exciting as it was going to be a little later.

When I got to Fourteenth Street, I got off and led my dinosaur across, just in case a car might be coming along. Then I climbed up again and we headed up the hill that leads to the monument. I could feel the dinosaur's shoulders moving under me, and I could see the big muscles of his legs and neck sliding around under his thick hide. When we reached the top of the hill I let Uncle Beazley have a little rest. The mist was thinning out some, and I could look across the Tidal Basin and see the Jefferson Memorial, but it was pretty faint in the gray light. I thought I would ride down toward the Tidal Basin and look at it closer. Everything went fine until I got to Independence Avenue, where Fifteenth Street crosses it. The traffic light was green, so I thought it would be safe to ride across and I started over. Uncle Beazley lumbered along, minding his own business, and when we were about halfway across the street a pickup truck came along and stopped just to the right of us. That made me kind of uneasy, for Uncle Beazley wasn't supposed to be seen in public if we could help it, and I wanted to get him out of sight as quickly as I could. But Uncle Beazley was so slow, the light changed on us before we made the other side of Independence Avenue. That was when the driver of the pickup made his big mistake. Instead of just waiting for us to move out of the way, he blew his horn, right in Uncle Beazley's ear almost.

Then Uncle Beazley went into action. He never did like horns being blown at him, and he swung right around and came over beside the pickup truck, and he put his big head down and just pitched that truck over onto its side as if it was no trouble at all. The driver climbed out the window and ran down the street yelling bloody murder.

I slid right off the dinosaur's back, and led him around to the other side of the truck and got him to lift it right side up again. Then I pulled hard on Uncle Beazley's rope and got him back across Independence Avenue as fast as I could. I couldn't see the truck driver around anywhere, so I headed back to the museum. I had a feeling there was going to be trouble, and I wanted to have Uncle Beazley safely back in his room when it started.

As soon as Dr. Ziemer came in I told him what had happened. He nodded his head.

"We had to expect something like that sooner or later," he said. "That dinosaur really isn't built to fit into modern traffic conditions. He has plenty of horsepower, but he doesn't have the speed. The Triceratops didn't have to depend on speed.

They were a quiet, stubborn type, and they liked to mind their own business until something tried to push them around, and then — watch out! They didn't have all that power for nothing, I can tell you." He looked over at me and chuckled. "People are like that too, sometimes, Nate. Particularly up where you come from."

"It would have been all right," I said, "if that man hadn't blown his horn right beside us. That was what did it. Uncle Beazley just turned right around and butted the truck over. If only people wouldn't blow horns that way."

The doctor smiled. " Horn-blowing is part of modern traffic, I guess. People pay good money for those horns, so they figure they have a right to use them."

"What do you suppose the police will do?" I wondered.

"I suspect they will tell us to keep our dinosaur off the streets, but we'd have to give up the morning walks anyway pretty soon, because the weather will be too cold. Don't worry, Nate," he said. "We'll handle this all right."

I couldn't help worrying some, though, because you never can be sure the police are going to understand about dinosaurs and things like that.

Chapter Fourteen

A LITTLE LATER THAT MORNING THE DIS-
trict of Columbia Police Department called on the telephone.

Dr. Ziemer took the call, and motioned me to listen in on
the other telephone. It was a pretty unusual conversation, so
I'll write it down here as close as I can remember it.

"Hello, Professor?" the voice said. "This is Captain Neeley
at the police station. We're just checking up on a report. A
man came in early this morning with a crazy story about a big
animal with horns. He said he was in his truck at Independence and Fifteenth, and saw this thing and thought it was
some sort of stuffed animal on wheels, but suddenly it turned
around and belted the truck right over on its side. He said he
climbed out the window and escaped and came in to report
to us. He said he thought he saw someone riding on it. It
looked like a kid, he said."

"Is that so?" Doctor Ziemer said, very calmly.

"I wouldn't have bothered you, Professor," the voice went on, "but the guy was perfectly sober, so we thought we'd better look into it. We went back to Independence and Fifteenth, and there was his truck all right, but it was right side up. The man couldn't explain that, but he swore up and down that when he left, that truck had been on its side. I was just going to take the guy back to the station for observation, when one of the men found a track over in the dirt near the sidewalk. It was a great big track about fourteen inches long, with four toes on it. I've never seen anything like it. We called the zoo, and they said it sounded like the track of an oversize tortoise, but their tortoise hadn't escaped, and besides, they didn't think a tortoise could turn over a truck."

"I think they're right," Dr. Ziemer said.

"But the zoo said to get in touch with you people at the museum, so I just wanted to ask if you had any idea what could have made that track."

"Why yes, I have a pretty good idea, Captain," Dr. Ziemer said. "I'm fairly certain that it was made by a Triceratops."

"A *what?*" the voice said.

"A Triceratops. A kind of a dinosaur. It has horns, just as the man said."

"All right, Professor." The captain's voice sounded a little sharp. "That truck was tipped over this morning, not a million years ago."

"I know that," the doctor said. "We heard the whole story from the boy who was riding the dinosaur."

There was a kind of pause at the other end of the telephone. "Would you repeat that, Professor? I didn't catch what you said."

"I said we heard about it from the boy who was riding the dinosaur."

Another pause. "I'm sorry, Professor, all I can hear is something that sounds like 'the boy was riding the dinosaur.' I guess our phone's on the blink."

"That's what I said," Dr. Ziemer said patiently. "We have a dinosaur, and the boy was out exercising it this morning when that — er — incident occurred."

Then there was an even longer pause. Finally the police captain said, "I'd better come over and see you about this," and then he hung up.

Later on the police captain came in. He was a tall man, and he had a big chin and looked very serious. Dr. Ziemer took him down in the basement and showed him Uncle Beazley.

"Holy smoke!" the police captain said. "How long have you had this thing here?"

"Almost three weeks," Dr. Ziemer told him.

"And you mean to say you've been letting him out every morning all this time? Why, that's dangerous. We can't allow a thing like this to wander around the public streets. There was no injury or property damage this morning when that truck was tipped over, but you may not be so lucky next time. You'll have to keep this animal locked up. No more traipsing around loose after this."

He frowned at Uncle Beazley through the gate and started to turn to go, but he turned around again quickly. "And another thing, Professor, there's a District ordinance against stabling large animals inside the District of Columbia limits except in designated areas." He took out a booklet and thumbed through it. "Cats and dogs, yes; rabbits, hamsters, guinea pigs, white rats, under certain conditions. No horses, cows, sheep, goats, pigs, or other livestock. No potentially dangerous animals, such as bear, leopard, raccoon, or ape, or the young of such animals, either caged or free. No reptiles. Doesn't even mention dinosaurs, Professor. I'm sorry. I'll give you twenty-four hours to clear him out of here. That's the best I can do for you." He wrote something in his notebook and snapped it shut, as if there was no use saying anything more about it. Then he walked out of the building.

"Well, Nate," Dr. Ziemer said, "what do we do now?" He rubbed his chin for a while. "I guess our best bet is the zoo. What do you say?"

I said I guessed that was all right with me, if they would take good care of Uncle Beazley.

"Oh, I'm sure they would," the doctor said. "He'd be their

prize exhibit and nothing would be too good for him. I'll call Holmquist at the zoo. He's a good friend of mine."

He talked on the phone for quite a while, and then he hung up and turned to me. "Holmquist said they would be very happy to have the dinosaur. They lost an elephant a while back and have an empty pen in the Elephant House. It would be just the thing for him. Big indoor room, heated; large outdoor pen for warm weather. Much better than his quarters here. There's only one difficulty," he said.

"What's that?" I said.

"The government." Dr. Ziemer leaned his chin in his hand. "There's a big economy drive on now. They do that every now and then. So there's a big squeeze on the Department of the Interior, and especially on the National Park Service. That's where the National Zoological Park comes in. Their budget has been cut way down. That's why they still have an empty elephant pen. Elephants eat too much. And so do dinosaurs, Nate. Holmquist says he wants your dinosaur like anything, but he's worried about his budget. He said to bring him over anyway, and we'd hope for the best."

The next morning early, Michael Finney brought around his truck and backed it up to the door of the museum. We loaded Uncle Beazley on pretty gently, because he weighed three thousand, one hundred and seventy-six pounds now, and was over seventeen feet long, and then we drove over to the

National Zoological Park. It was only about two or three miles. We went up Connecticut Avenue, and then turned off into Rock Creek Park. Then the truck climbed up the hill to the Elephant House, past a sign that said:

LOST ARTICLES AND CHILDREN WILL
BE TAKEN TO THE LION HOUSE.

I thought that was pretty rough on the children, because it must be kind of easy to get lost in a big zoo like that.

We drove around to the back of the Elephant House, and Mr. Holmquist met us there. They had a ramp, and they moved that up to the back of the truck, and we eased Uncle Beazley out backwards. It was slow work, but we finally managed it. Then I led him into the inner pen, and showed him the water trough and the feed rack. Then I showed him around the outer pen. From his pen he could see the hippopotamuses and the giraffes, so he wouldn't be too lonely. The keeper put in a big pile of alfalfa and feed, and Uncle Beazley started right in on it.

"We'll come up every day to measure and weigh him," Dr. Ziemer said, and then we thanked Mr. Holmquist and drove away in the truck.

"So far, so good," the doctor said. "Now we'll wait and see what Congress does when they hear about it."

I think it was about three days later that Mr. Holmquist called the museum, and told us that a Congressional committee was coming out to the zoo to look into the question of the dinosaur. "You better come right over to answer questions about your animal," he suggested.

Uncle Beazley was in fine shape when we got there. He'd put on a lot more weight, as usual, and was rubbing his shoulder against the bars in a very comfortable way. Dr. Ziemer nudged me and pointed to a group of four men that had just walked in. They took a quick look around the room and walked right over toward the dinosaur cage.

"This must be the one, over here," one of the men said. He had a bald head and smoked a cigar. The other men gathered around and stared at Uncle Beazley. A keeper came along and tossed three bags of alfalfa and a bag of grain into his hopper.

"How long does he take to eat that feed?" the man with the cigar said.

"Oh, he finishes all that up in half an hour," the keeper said. "He's got a real appetite, that boy. He takes eight sacks of

alfalfa and two hundred pounds of grain every day. It does your heart good just to watch him eat."

"Did you hear that, Ed?" the man with the cigar said. "That's where the money goes."

"What do they call that kind of an animal, anyway?" another of the men said.

Dr. Ziemer stepped forward. "That's a Triceratops, gentlemen," he told them.

"I've never seen anything like that around anywhere," another man said. "Where'd he come from?"

"From the town of Freedom, New Hampshire," Dr. Ziemer told him. "This boy here raised him from the time he was hatched."

"Kind of an ugly brute, isn't he?" the man said. "Is there any particular reason for keeping him here at the taxpayers' expense?"

"Well, he's the only animal of his kind in the world, as far as we know," Dr. Ziemer said. "We think it's very important that scientists be able to study such a rare specimen as this. It's a wonderful thing for Americans to have a live Triceratops right here in the National Zoo."

"I don't know about that," the man with the cigar said. "It's time that people learned that the United States Government isn't going to pay for every fool notion that turns up." He pointed his cigar at Dr. Ziemer and me. "I'd like you two to come to the Senate Office Building tomorrow at eleven A.M. I want to look into this little matter of your dinosaur. Senator Granderson's office." He turned around and walked out of the Elephant House, with the other men following him.

Chapter Fifteen

IN THE MORNING DR. ZIEMER AND I WENT UP
to the Senate Office Building. It's a big building right next to
the Capitol, where the Senators work and figure things out
when they're not in the Senate making laws and speeches and
things like that. We found Senator Granderson's office on the
second floor, and walked in. After we had waited around for
a while a secretary told us to step in to the inner office.

Senator Granderson was sitting in the middle of a cloud of
cigar smoke, and he got up and shook Dr. Ziemer's hand, and
he shook my hand, and then he pointed to some chairs for us
to sit in. He sat down again behind a great big desk with a
glass top.

Senator Granderson cleared his throat and leaned back in
his chair. "Now, gentlemen," he said, "I want you to understand that I have no personal objections to this dinosaur. I
have no doubt it is an excellent animal, ah — in its own way.

151

My only interest in the matter is to save money for the tax-payers. My committee is trying very hard to find ways of cutting down the expenses of the government. We want to get rid of anything that isn't absolutely necessary to the welfare of the American people. And right here in the District of Columbia, in our own National Zoological Park, we find a big expensive animal eating up feed by the ton. Now I ask you, gentlemen, how is a Tyrannosaur like that going to help the welfare of the American people?"

"Triceratops," Dr. Ziemer said.

"All right, Doctor," Senator Granderson said. "You can call it anything you like, but the point is, what good is it?"

"But Senator," Dr. Ziemer said, "you might just as well ask what good is an elephant? They're expensive to feed too."

"Oh, elephants are quite another matter," the Senator said.

"An elephant is a standard, well-recognized animal. You read about them in books and you see them in the circus. They are a solid part of our wholesome American tradition. The elephant has become a symbol of one of our great political parties. But of course you can have too many of them. One elephant is enough for a zoo. No need to have more than one."

"But Senator, there are different kinds of elephants," Dr. Ziemer said. "There are Indian elephants and African elephants, for instance. Don't you think the public should have a chance to see more than one kind of elephant?"

"Now Doctor," the Senator said, patting his big hand on the desk, "an elephant is an elephant, and that's all that the man on the street needs to know. If it's in an American zoo, it's an American elephant, so why should he worry where it comes from? But I want to get back to this dinosaur of yours. Where did you get it from?"

Dr. Ziemer nodded to me, so I answered the question. "It came from our chicken yard," I told him.

"And where is that?" the Senator wanted to know.

"Up in Freedom, New Hampshire."

"I see," the Senator said. "And just what was this animal doing in your chicken yard?"

"One of our hens laid it. She was part Rhode Island Red and part Barred Plymouth Rock."

The Senator raised his eyebrows. "You mean to tell me that

this Pterodac — this dinosaur hatched out of a *hen's* egg? That sounds mighty suspicious to me. Are you sure someone didn't slip this egg into your henhouse when you weren't looking? Did you see any suspicious characters around your place at the time?"

"Yes — I mean no," I said, because I wasn't quite sure what question I was answering. "But anyway," I said, "the hen hatched it out. She sat on it faithfully for six weeks. It was a long job."

But Senator Granderson wasn't listening. He sat frowning down at his desk top for a while. Then he looked up at Dr. Ziemer.

"You ever seen any dinosaur eggs before, Doctor?"

"Oh, yes," Dr. Ziemer said. "We have many of them."

"Where'd they come from?" the Senator wanted to know.

"From the Gobi Desert, in Outer Mongolia," Dr. Ziemer said. "But those were eggs of the Protoceratops andrewsi — "

The Senator thumped his fist down on the desk. "Gentlemen," he said, "I know now what I must do. My duty is clear. This animal does not belong in our National Zoological Park. He is not an American animal, and our National Zoo is no place for him. We must not maintain foreign freaks at the public expense. Lions, tigers, giraffes — all the proper animals, yes. But no un-American, outmoded creatures from foreign places. The dinosaurs are extinct, aren't they? Do you want people to get the false idea that such things still exist, right here in America?"

"But Senator — " Dr. Ziemer said.

Senator Granderson raised his big hand. "No, Doctor," he said. "Don't attempt to dissuade me. I see my duty. Today in the Senate I shall propose legislation to make it unlawful to keep any out-of-date, unusual, or unlikely animals in the National Zoo or in the National Parks or anywhere within the borders of the United States or its possessions." He got up from his chair and walked over to the door and opened it for us. "I will be very busy now, gentlemen, so I must say good-by. Thank you for your time."

The next thing we knew, Dr. Ziemer and I were out in the corridor. The doctor stared down at the floor, and he looked pretty discouraged. "Well, Nate," he said, "things don't look very bright for Uncle Beazley. Perhaps it would have been better if we'd just let him stay up in New Hampshire. It's really my fault for getting him into this difficulty."

"It isn't your fault, Dr. Ziemer," I said. "You were trying to do the best thing you could for him. You didn't know that things would turn out this way."

Dr. Ziemer and I went back to the Museum. The doctor sat down on the edge of his desk and stared out the window. Then he got up and walked back and forth on the rug, with his hands jammed down in his pockets.

Finally he stopped and turned to me. "I always feel so help-less when I get tangled up with Congress," he said. "I just don't understand how their minds work. I know an Archaeop-teryx when I see one, and I can tell an Ichthyosaur from a Plesiosaur, or a Trilobite from a Graptolite, but I don't know anything about Senators."

"Why do you suppose Senator Granderson doesn't like dino-saurs?" I asked him. "What's he got against them?"

Dr. Ziemer shrugged his shoulders. "I haven't any idea. He just gets a whim every now and then — usually just before elections — that he's got to do something to save the country. Last year he was going to save the country from comic books. Maybe you heard about that. The year before it was firecrack-ers. Next year it will be basketball, or outboard motors. You never can tell what it will be next. And the strange thing is that he can get people so excited that they think he's right. He got everyone so worked up about cap pistols that now they're illegal in every state except Nevada and Idaho, and they use nothing but real guns there anyway. One time he proposed a law to get rid of all the buffalo on the government ranges out West, and he almost got it through the Senate."

After lunch Dr. Ziemer took me to the gallery above the Senate, and we found some seats right down by the front, where we could look over the railing and see just about every-thing that was going on down below us. One of the Senators was making a speech about American broadleaf tobacco, but I didn't listen to him much because I was worrying about what was going to happen to Uncle Beazley. Pretty soon Dr. Ziemer nudged me, and I looked down and saw Senator Granderson walking into the room. The man who was talking about tobacco finally sat down, and the other Senators clapped a little, but not very hard.

The next thing I knew, Senator Granderson was standing up beside his desk. "Mr. President," he said in a big booming voice, "I wish to speak today about a subject that affects us all. My fellow Senators all know me as one who has constantly devoted himself to the welfare and safety of the American people, and I am sure they will listen carefully as I describe a situation which is not only a needless expense to the American taxpayer, but which also constitutes a grave danger to every man, woman, and child in this great land of ours." He paused for a while and looked around the room as if he expected everybody to clap.

"I need not remind you that our government is trying to reduce its topheavy budget, and to lower the staggering tax burden that strains the backs of all American citizens. I myself have spent many weary hours seeking out waste and unnecessary expense in the various branches of our Federal establishment. You can imagine my dismay when I discovered an example of such waste right here in our national capital. I am grieved to say this, gentlemen, but right here in our National Zoological Park is an animal that is squandering the taxpayer's hard-earned money at the disgraceful rate of twenty-one dollars and sixty cents a day, every day of the week, Saturdays and Sundays included. And what is more, gentlemen, this animal is absolutely worthless. It does no honest work, it pulls no plow, it grows no wool. And what is even *more*, gentlemen, this animal I speak of is no normal creature like the lions and tigers and elephants that roam the woods and plains of our fair country — " Someone nudged the Senator when he said this and leaned over and whispered with him. "Of our fair country, I say," Senator Granderson went on, "or the woods and plains of our sister nations across the seas. No decent, ordinary, up-to-date animal is this, gentlemen, but a queer, freakish survivor of a race that died out millions of years ago, perhaps *hundreds* of millions of years ago."

"That's stretching it pretty far," Dr. Ziemer whispered to me. "Seventy million years is the most I can allow him for the Triceratops. They were no earlier than the Late Mesozoic."

The Senator raised his big hand over his head, and waggled a finger at the other Senators the way Miss Watkins does, when she's getting ready to scold us in class. "The animal I speak of is a *dinosaur*, gentlemen, of the type known as the Tyranno — ah, rather, I should say the Triplo — no, that's not it . . . The scientific name escapes me at the moment,

gentlemen, but it makes no difference what we call it, it still is the ugliest, evilest-looking reptilian I have ever seen, and it's a disgrace to our National Zoological Park and to the department that operates it. Can you imagine *for one moment* bringing the innocent, bright-eyed children of good American families to look at this inefficient, outmoded and outlandish specimen of a bygone age? Do we want our children to grow up to be forward-looking citizens of our forward-looking country? Then we must not let them dwell on the useless creatures of the past, the foolish mistakes of Nature discarded long before Columbus planted the American flag on our beautiful shores. No, gentlemen, there must be no living in the past for us, but rather we must bravely face the future, and march on together, hand in hand and shoulder to shoulder, to that glorious destiny that lies before us."

Some of the Senators clapped, and Senator Granderson took a few swallows of water from a glass on his table.

"I propose to get rid of this monster," Senator Granderson went on. "I am submitting a bill before the Senate to make the possession of all such unnatural animals a Federal offense. He should be exterminated and the sooner the better."

Another man near Senator Granderson stood up. "I agree with the honorable Senator, and I want to propose an amendment to his bill. I propose that this dinosaur be skinned and stuffed, and presented to Senator Granderson as a trophy in recognition of his untiring work in searching out waste and error in the national government."

I pulled Dr. Ziemer's sleeve when I heard that. "Would they really do that to Uncle Beazley?" I asked him in a whisper.

"Not if we can help it, Nate," Dr. Ziemer said.

Then another Senator got up. "What does this dinosaur eat?" he wanted to know.

"It eats grain and alfalfa," Senator Granderson told him. "Tremendous amounts of it. And he is growing bigger and bigger, and he eats more every day. Soon we shall all be starving just to satisfy the appetite of the gluttonous beast." He slapped his fat stomach to kind of emphasize what he said.

"Well," the other Senator said, in a sort of a drawly voice, "my constituents in Nebraska would be happy to have him eat all the alfalfa he wants, Senator. Why wouldn't it be a good idea to feed him government stores of surplus grain and alfalfa? We could feed the animal for years on that, and it wouldn't cost us a cent. We've been trying to think of some way to use up all that surplus. How about that?"

"Never!" Senator Granderson roared. "I wouldn't dream of *giving* away this surplus food to an ugly beast, when the hardworking American housewife has to *buy* it with her hardearned money."

"The American housewife doesn't eat much alfalfa, Senator," a man called from the back row. There was a lot of laughter, and the Vice President had to knock on his desk to quiet things down.

Well, the arguments went on this way for a long time, and nobody seemed to be getting anywhere. Dr. Ziemer didn't look very happy, and he kept shaking his head every now and then.

"Nate," he said, "I don't know how this is going to come out, but the Senators will probably go on making speeches at each other until midnight, and then there won't be enough of them here to take a vote, so they'll postpone it until tomorrow. We might as well go home and get some sleep."

We got up and went out. Dr. Ziemer didn't say anything all the way back to the apartment and he just walked along looking at the sidewalk. I could tell that he was worried, and that made *me* worried.

After I'd crawled into bed the doctor came in to say good night to me. He sat down on the edge of the bed after I turned out the light. He didn't say anything, and he just sat there, looking kind of tired and discouraged.

"I guess there isn't much hope for Uncle Beazley," I said, trying to sound calm, but my voice came out a little quivery.

"Well, we won't give up till we have to," he said. "It doesn't look too good for us, but we may think of something yet."

I sat up in bed suddenly. "Do you think we could slip over

to the zoo with the truck, and load Uncle Beazley into it, and sneak him away and hide him somewhere? They couldn't kill him if they couldn't find him, could they?"

The doctor shook his head. "It would be pretty hard to hide anything so big, Nate. A Triceratops wasn't really made for running away from things. When something attacked him, he would meet the trouble head on. That's why a Triceratops has all those horns and armor plate on the front end. And he was a tough customer, too. Even the Tyrannosaur would think twice about taking on a Triceratops. Maybe we'd better take a lesson from Uncle Beazley. I don't think we'd get anywhere trying to run away from the trouble. It would catch up with us sooner or later. We'll keep thinking. But it's terribly late. You get to sleep now or you'll never wake up till lunchtime."

He closed the door softly behind him. I didn't go to sleep for a long time, trying to think of some way to save Uncle Beazley. I could hear Dr. Ziemer walking up and down in the next room. He was still walking when I went to sleep.

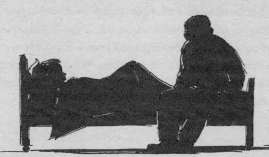

Chapter Sixteen

WHEN I WOKE UP THE NEXT MORNING I had that kind of gloomy feeling you get when you think something bad is likely to happen. I tried to go back to sleep again, but I couldn't. I looked up at the calendar on the wall, where I'd been crossing off the days. Today was Wednesday, October 2, and that meant I would have to go back to school in five more days. And then I thought that if they were going to kill Uncle Beazley, I wouldn't want to stay around here when they did *that*. And so I'd better go back home to Freedom, and go back to school, and just try to forget about the whole thing. But it would be awful going back to school *before* I was supposed to, and everyone would ask what the matter was, and I'd have to keep *explaining* to people all the time, and I sure wouldn't enjoy that very much. When everything has gone all wrong, and the luck's all against you, you don't feel like going around talking about it.

Well, I went in to see if Dr. Ziemer was awake, and he was shaving.

"Good morning, Nate," he said. "How about running down to the store and getting a quart of milk and a loaf of bread? And while you're at it, pick up a newspaper, will you? I want to see how Senator Granderson is getting along."

I was back in a few minutes. The doctor was setting the table.

"Read me the news while I make the toast," he said. He stuck a fork into a slice of bread and held it over the gas flame on the stove. I turned to the news about Congress.

DINOSAUR BILL DEBATED IN SENATE

WASHINGTON, October 4

The Senate wrangled until a late hour last night over the bill proposed by Senator Granderson. This bill, if made law, will outlaw all dinosaurs from the United States. Senator Tarboy spoke in favor of the bill, and proposed an amendment to the effect that the present dinosaur be stuffed at government expense and presented to Senator Granderson. Senator Tarboy is a member of the Committee on Economy in the Government. Senator Granderson said he objected to the dinosaur because it was wasting the taxpayers' money, and because it was inefficient and out of date. "Our country has no use for things that have become extinct," Senator Granderson declared.

A small group of Senators have protested the "Dinosaur Bill," as it is called, but they have made little headway. Unless something unforeseen happens in the next two or three days, it is very likely that the Dinosaur Bill will pass both houses, and the world's only living dinosaur will go to join his extinct ancestors.

The doctor didn't say anything for a while. He finished buttering the toast, and then he poured out his coffee and stirred it with the butter knife. I had the only spoon, because I needed it for my eggs. We kept meaning to buy another spoon and fork, but we only thought of it at breakfast times. "But don't worry about me," Dr. Ziemer said. "Out in the field on fossil-hunting expeditions I've stirred my coffee with everything from toothbrushes to screwdrivers, and the coffee always tastes just the same."

He took a swallow of coffee, and then he pointed to the paper. "Doesn't look at all good, does it? Well, I didn't think Congress would help us much anyway."

"I guess that's about the end of it, then," I said. I swallowed a few times and then I said, "I might as well start packing my suitcase. I don't want to be around when they take Uncle Beazley out and shoot him."

"Hold on, Nate," the doctor said. "We're not going to give up *that* easily. We still have another card to play."

"What is it?" I said. "Do you mean we might steal him away from the zoo like the way I said last night?"

"No, no, Nate. We must be legal about this. I think we've got a much better way than that. What is it that keeps a Senator going, do you think?"

"His lungs, I guess," I said.

"Well, that helps all right — but what's he got to have before he can ever get *into* the Senate?"

I couldn't see what he was driving at. "I give up. What's he got to have?"

"Why, *votes*," the doctor said. "Unless people vote for him, a Senator is nothing at all."

"Well, I didn't vote for Senator Granderson," I said. "But he's right in there, just the same. And I can't tell other people how to vote can I?"

"*That's* just it," Dr. Ziemer said. "I think you *can* tell them."

"Who, me? I'm not old enough to vote myself."

"But you're old enough to ask people to write to their Congressmen." Dr. Ziemer looked over at me, and poured himself another cup of coffee.

I didn't think much of *that* idea. How was I going to tell all these people to write their Congressmen? What was I going to do — stand out on the street corner and shout to everybody? I didn't see how that was going to work, and I told Dr. Ziemer so.

"No, you don't have to stand on the street corner," he said. "You can tell them on TV. I know a man named Bonelli, who has a little television program every week. It's called Capital Sidelight. He tries to show people all over the country what's going on here in Washington, and he gets people that are in the news to speak on his program. It's pretty good."

"But what's that got to do with us?" I said.

"It has *everything* to do with us. Mr. Bonelli called me up this morning while you were out, and he wondered if you would like to give a little talk on his show. He wanted to have something about the Dinosaur Bill this week, and since you've known the dinosaur better than anyone else, you're the logical person to talk about it."

I gulped. "But I've never *been* on a TV show before. I wouldn't know what to do."

"Oh, that's all right," Dr. Ziemer said. "It's perfectly simple. And, remember, it may be our only chance to save Uncle Beazley."

"But couldn't *you* do the talking?" I asked him. "You'd know what to say and everything. You could tell them how important Uncle Beazley was for science."

"I'm afraid that wouldn't work, Nate. People don't really care what happens to Science. And they're not going to take much trouble to save a dinosaur just so a lot of silly scientists can study him. But if it's a matter of taking a boy's pet away from him — well, they can get pretty excited about that. As far as I can see, you're Uncle Beazley's only hope."

I thought about that for a while. I just couldn't *imagine* talking on a television program, but if I had to do it to save my dinosaur — well, then I just *had* to do it.

"Okay," I said. "I — I guess I can try, anyhow."

"Fine," the doctor said. "Now, Mr. Bonelli wanted us to come over to his studio this morning, and we could talk over what you are going to say on the program. All right?"

"Y-yes," I said, but I wasn't any too sure about it.

We went over to the studio, and a secretary showed us into Mr. Bonelli's office. He was a short, quick little man, and he kept walking up and down the room all the time. He shook hands with me and had me sit down in a big leather chair.

"Now, then," he said, walking back and forth all the time he was talking, "I understand you used to keep this dinosaur in your back yard."

I nodded.

"Was he fierce? Did he ever try to hurt you?"

"Oh, no," I said. "He was just as gentle as anything. He just ate and slept and walked around. Only he was a little shy with other people."

"But I understand you had some trouble with a truck here in Washington. Is that right?"

"That was because the truck driver was in such a hurry that

he blew his horn right in the dinosaur's ear. He never did like it when people blew their — "

"I see," Mr. Bonelli said. "Was he expensive to feed?"

"Not while we fed him on grass. That didn't cost us anything up in Freedom. It just grows wild all around there."

"That was Freedom, New Hampshire, wasn't it? Tell me about your family. Got any brothers or sisters? What does your father do? How do you like Washington?"

He went on asking questions like that, and I answered them the best I could. Finally he stopped and held up his hand.

"All right," he said. "I guess that gives us enough to go on. Now, I'll work this up into a little talk for you, and have the secretary type it up, and you can read it when your turn comes in the program. You come around at about seven this evening, and that will give you time to read over your talk and get all set."

"Is the program *tonight?*" I groaned. "Gosh, I won't even have time enough to *worry* about it."

Mr. Bonelli laughed and showed us out of the office.

Well, I had one awful day. Whenever I thought about talking on the TV show I got cold shivers down my back, and my stomach would go all queer. I couldn't hardly eat any lunch, what with thinking about the program, and what would happen if I got all mixed up and couldn't say things straight. I never was any good at public speaking. I only had a couple of crackers for supper, and *they* didn't set any too easy.

"Everybody gets that way before their first speech," Dr. Ziemer told me. "Just remember that once you start talking everything will be all right. The bad part is *before* the talking."

We got over to the studio, and Mr. Bonelli gave me a typewritten sheet and we read it over together. It was a pretty good speech, I guess — better than I could do — but it wasn't *my* speech. Somehow it didn't seem quite right for me to talk somebody else's words like that. And it didn't say anything about how I wanted to save Uncle Beazley. Mr. Bonelli had me read it a few times, and he told me to be sure to talk slowly and clearly, and then he looked at his watch and said we ought to be in the studio at five minutes to eight. My stomach sort of caved in when I heard that, but I swallowed hard and kind of nodded to him, and he went out.

Dr. Ziemer looked over at me and smiled. "That speech isn't quite what you wanted to say, is it?"

"No," I said. "I guess not."

"What do you *really* want to tell them? Do you know?"

"Well, sure," I said. "I want to tell them that I like my dinosaur and that I'm trying to save him, and they can help if they all tell their Congressmen that they don't want the Dinosaur Bill."

"Good," Dr. Ziemer said. "As long as you know what you really want to say, everything will be all right."

I didn't see what he meant by that — at least not until later. The doctor came over to me and picked up my paper. He looked at it for a while, and then he walked into the next room with it. He came back again in a minute and handed me the paper all folded up.

"Put it in your pocket until the program begins," he said. I put it in my pocket, and a few minutes later Mr. Bonelli stuck his head in the door.

"Let's go," he said. I followed him into the studio, and we sat down at a table. There was a big camera on wheels, and some awful bright lights that made me blink. Mr. Bonelli pointed to an electric clock on the wall. It was about two minutes before eight.

"We begin at eight," he said, "and your part comes about ten minutes later. Are you all set? Got your speech?"

I put my hand in my pocket, and I felt the paper, and I nodded to him.

Mr. Bonelli turned toward the camera and smiled and just as the red second hand on the clock touched twelve, he started talking.

"Good evening, friends," he said, in a sort of smooth voice. "This is Ben Bonelli, bringing you this week's Capital Sidelight, fifteen minutes of news and views of the political scene here at your nation's capital. First of all, about our distinguished visitor from Peru. Señor Gasparillo Mendoza arrived by plane yesterday afternoon, and was greeted at the airport — "

I was too worried about myself to hear the rest of what Mr. Bonelli said. I took the paper out of my pocket and opened it up. For a minute I just stared at it. There wasn't any speech there at all! It was just a blank paper with a few words written in pencil. All it said was: "You know what to say, Nate. Go ahead and make your own speech."

Well, I could have sunk through the floor. Here it was almost time for me to read my speech and I didn't *have* any speech to read. At first I thought I'd better crawl under the rug and hide or maybe make a dash for the door. My hands felt like ice, and they shook so I could hardly hold onto the paper.

And then I heard Mr. Bonelli say, " — and we have him here in the studio with us tonight. This is Nathan Twitchell, the young man from Freedom, New Hampshire, who raised this dinosaur from the time it was hatched. Well, Nathan, would you like to say a few words to our audience?" Then he turned around and looked straight at me.

My stomach flipped upside down and started climbing up in my throat. I opened my mouth, but I couldn't get any words to come out. And then I thought that if I didn't say something pretty quick, there wouldn't be any more Uncle Beazley. That big old dinosaur depended on *me*, so I just *had* to start talking.

So I looked straight at the camera and took a deep breath and just said the first thing that came into my head.

"Hello," I said. Out of the corner of my eye I could see Mr. Bonelli making signals for me to get going. Of course he didn't know what the matter was, but I couldn't tell him, right in the middle of the program like that.

"Er — hello, everybody," I said. "I'm Nate Twitchell, and I live up in New Hampshire, and one morning last summer I found this big egg in our chickenhouse, and when it hatched out it was a dinosaur, and I took care of him, and fed him

grass all summer, and he got to be awful tame and friendly with me. But we couldn't keep him up there over the winter because he needed a warm place, and besides he was getting pretty big for our little town, so we brought him down here to Washington. And then we gave him to the zoo because they've got just the right place for him, and people could come in and see him. And then when I thought everything was all set, some men in Congress thought they'd save money by getting rid of the dinosaur. They said he wasn't American, and he was no good for anything. But that's not right. I found out at the museum that America's the only country that ever *had* horned dinosaurs. They were all living out in Wyoming sixty million years ago, and that was before even the Pilgrims landed, I guess."

I could see Mr. Bonelli wiggling his hands and trying to get me to read the speech he'd written for me. I figured I'd better hurry up before he stopped me.

"And besides, I took care of that dinosaur, and I fed him, and I watched him grow big and strong, and I sure would hate to have him killed. I know he does eat a lot, but maybe he's worth it, because he's the only dinosaur we've got. He isn't any beauty, but I like him a lot. And I — I was just hoping that some of you people that are listening would want to save my dinosaur, though now he's really *your* dinosaur too, and if you *do* want to save him, would you *please* tell your

Senators and Representatives to vote against the Dinosaur Bill. But you better do it quick or there won't be anything left to save."

Mr. Bonelli broke in before I could say any more. He leaned over to his microphone and said, "Well, Nate, that was very interesting. We hope you enjoy Washington while you're here. Now, that's all for this evening, folks. Be sure to tune in again next Thursday to Capital Sidelight, the program that brings you the people in the news in your nation's capital."

The clock said exactly fifteen minutes after eight when he finished. Mr. Bonelli turned to me and said, "Why in — in the name of goodness didn't you read the speech I gave you?"

"I couldn't find it," I said. "When I opened up the paper, it was just blank."

"Well, look in your pockets. The speech must be there."

I went through all my pockets, but no speech.

"You kids are always losing things," Mr. Bonelli said. "Every time I have a kid on my program, I swear that I'll never do it again. You give a kid a paper, and thirty seconds later he's lost it, and the funny thing is *you can't ever find it again*. What they do with them is a mystery to me."

Dr. Ziemer came over and took me by the arm. "I think Nate did very well," he said. "He had to make up his talk as he went along."

"Oh sure, sure," Mr. Bonelli said. "It was a fine speech, but it wasn't the one I wrote for him. I was going to have him just tell about his family, and his town, and what the dinosaur was like, and so on. I don't like to get tangled up with controversial issues in this program."

"Yes, I know," Dr. Ziemer said. We said good-by and went back to the apartment. When we got there, Dr. Ziemer took a piece of paper out of his pocket and gave it to me. I opened it up. It was the speech Mr. Bonelli wrote for me!

"Where'd you find this?" I asked him.

"Oh, I kept it, and gave you a blank paper in exchange. Mr. Bonelli's speech wouldn't have saved Uncle Beazley, but I think yours will. I kept this one so you'd have to make your own, and you did. It was a good speech."

"Well, you sure gave me some bad moments. I almost passed out when I saw that blank sheet."

He smiled and patted me on the back. "I know, Nate. It was a terrible spot to put you in, but I couldn't think of any better way. Now let's hope it works."

Nothing much happened until noon the next day. That was when we got a telephone call from Dr. Kennedy.

"Say," he said, "that talk on TV was just the thing! I hear that telegrams have been coming in all morning. They've been coming in by the basketload. The whole Senate's flooded with telegrams, even all the way from Utah and

Texas. And they all say 'Save that dinosaur.' If things keep on this way, the Dinosaur Bill's going to fall flat on its face."

Dr. Ziemer put down the telephone and broke into the broadest grin you ever saw, and then he jumped up and grabbed me by the arms, and we went sashaying round and round his desk. Right in the middle of it the phone rang again.

"Hello?" the doctor said.

"Hello, Ziemer," the voice said. "This is Holmquist, at the zoo. Say, what's going on, anyway? A whole crowd of people suddenly descended on us from Baltimore. They had some banners and signs that read 'Save the Dinosaur!' and they all marched up to the Elephant House and paraded around, and they said they were going to do twenty-four-hour guard duty to protect the dinosaur, and then about six busloads of people from Richmond came in, and *they* all had banners, and they piled into the Elephant House, and then there was a big crowd from Charlottesville, and top of all that a whole lot of people from the Parent-Teacher Association of Fairfax County arrived, and they all had flags, and everybody's getting all tangled up and the place is a madhouse. The giraffes don't know what to make of it."

"Don't worry, Holmquist," the doctor said. "Just tell the giraffes that it's a demonstration of sound American principles, and everything's all right." Then he hung up and we went on dancing around the desk.

In a few minutes the phone rang again. It was Mr. Holmquist. "What do I do now, Ziemer?" he said. "There's a delegation here representing all the elementary school children of Arlington County, and they have two hundred and seventeen dollars all in nickels and pennies, and they want to give it to the zoo so we can buy the dinosaur's food with it. What shall I do about it?"

"Accept it," Dr. Ziemer said. "And I suggest that you set up a barrel with a sign on it, saying 'Contributions to Dinosaur Food Fund.' Better make it a good-sized barrel too."

Well, by the next morning things were really humming. They called up from the Senate Office Building and said that so much mail had come in that they were handling it with snow shovels, and the Senators were all backing water as fast as they could and saying that they had never really been in favor of the Dinosaur Bill at all. Up at the zoo Mr. Holmquist was having a fit. He'd never seen such a crowd there before, and the Elephant House had been jammed with people ever since opening time. Thirteen children had been lost by lunchtime, and eighteen hundred dollars and forty-three cents had been put in the barrel the last time they counted. Delegations had come from the Warrenton Girl Scouts, the League of Women Voters of Casanova and Hagerstown and Chambersburg, and the United Boys' Club of Bumpass and Beaverdam, Virginia. The whole Brandywine Bird Watchers' Society came, and the Mechanicsville Fife and Drum Corps, and the Citizens' Committee for Secondary Schools from Point of Rocks.

It went on all day like that, and Dr. Ziemer looked as pleased as punch, and kept on chuckling to himself.

"You know, Nate," he said, "people are funny. Just think of all those thousands of people crowding into Washington to give all that money to save our dinosaur. You'd think that a live dinosaur was the one thing that Americans wanted above everything else. And yet if Senator Granderson hadn't tried to get rid of the dinosaur, none of those people would have given a hoot about it. I guess they don't get excited about a thing until somebody starts taking it away from them. Then they wake up and fight for it. It's like fishing, isn't it? Sometimes you don't get a bite until you start to take in the line."

Chapter Seventeen

WELL, FINALLY I HAD TO GO HOME. I WAS having a neat time in Washington, but Mr. Jenkins had said I could only stay out of school four weeks, and my time was up. I went down to the zoo to see Uncle Beazley for the last time, and I scratched his neck with a rake the way he likes, and I said good-by to him, but he probably didn't understand what I meant. He was getting to be awful big, but he was still gentle and friendly with me. Mr. Holmquist said they'd take specially good care of him, and Dr. Ziemer said he would send me a bulletin every week about how Uncle Beazley was getting along. I was glad to have him in such good hands.

Dr. Ziemer said good-by to me at the station. Just before the train left he gave me a fossil dinosaur egg, in a special wooden box just to fit it.

"All of us at the museum thought you ought to have this to keep," he said, "in return for what you've done for us and all the other scientists all over the world. Now good-by, Nate, and be sure to come back and see us again, won't you?"

"You bet," I said. "And — and thanks ever so much, Dr. Ziemer — " But then the train started, and all I could do was wave to him until he was out of sight.

When the train pulled into Ashland, New Hampshire, there were Pop and Mom and Cynthia waiting at the station. When I stepped off the train they all hugged me at once, even Cynthia. I didn't mind, though, because there was no one else around but the station agent, and he was eating his lunch and didn't notice.

There was a kind of parade when I got back to Freedom, and they had me ride down the street in the Champignys' truck, and there was a big sign on the grocery store that said WELCOME HOME NATE TWITCHELL on it, and the school band played some music, all five of them marching together in front of the truck. The parade went all the way up to the school-house, and Mr. Jenkins came out and very kindly handed me my schoolbooks, even though I wasn't in any great hurry about them, and I could have easily waited until the next day. Then the parade turned around and came back to our house. As soon as the truck stopped I got down, because I felt pretty

foolish up there with everybody looking at me, though I liked it, too, in a way. Mom and Cynthia had a table out in front of the house, and they served cider and doughnuts to the whole crowd.

It was one of those terrific days that you get sometimes up here in October. The sky was so blue you could hardly believe it, and everywhere you looked you could see all those bright

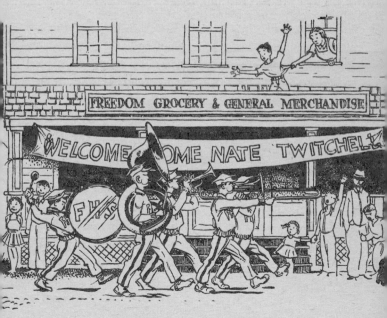

red and yellow leaves against the sky. It looked as if Nature had put everything she had into making one really perfect day. Even the smells were perfect — a mixture of smoke from across the street, and that dry smell of leaves on the ground, and the smell of warm grass and dirt in the sunshine, and just on the edge of it all, the faintest whiff of sweet cider.

The excitement died down pretty fast, and the next day I went to school, and I had to study subjects and predicates and fractions just as if I'd never been away at all. And now one day goes along pretty much like another, and there's not much excitement. There's plenty to do, though, what with laying in the stovewood for the winter, and taking care of the goat and the chickens. It gets dark out by suppertime now, and we sit around the stove evenings, and the warmth feels good.

Once a week, though, a letter comes from Dr. Ziemer down in Washington. He keeps me posted on how Uncle Beazley is coming along. The latest letter I had said that he was almost twenty feet long and weighed thirteen thousand nine hundred pounds. The doctor said that Uncle Beazley was not growing so fast now, and that probably meant he wasn't a baby any more, and he could take his time about reaching his full size. "He still has another few feet to add to his length," Dr. Ziemer wrote, "and another three tons to his weight. But he probably won't be full-grown for fifty years, and he may live for a hundred years after that. If all goes well, your little pet will be an ornament to the National Zoological Park for a long, long time. He is eating well — about four hundred pounds of feed a day — but we don't need to worry about the expense. Visitors have contributed $240,271.31 by closing time today (January 28), and money is still coming in fast. Even if we have no more contributions from now on, the dinosaur's food bill is paid all the way through 1996, and if the Congress threatens to get rid of him then, you could come down and make another speech for us. So I guess the wonderful American dinosaur is safe for a while, anyway."

Well, I guess that's about the end of the story. After cold weather settled in, Pop suggested that I ought to write it all down in a sort of a book, and so I did. I wrote some every evening after supper at the kitchen table, and it used up the most tremendous pile of paper, and it was an awful lot of work and I'm glad it's all over. Pop says I better not show it to Miss Watkins, or I'd be writing out spelling mistakes until I'm old enough to vote. Miss Watkins is my teacher, and she gets pretty worked up about spelling and commas, and things like that.

We never got in our camping trip to Franconia Notch, but Mom thinks maybe we could go to Washington during the spring vacation. I could show them all the sights, but most of the time I want to be up at the zoo, keeping up my friendship with Uncle Beazley. And if you're in Washington, D. C., in the spring, and if you happen to go into the Elephant House and look in the dinosaur cage, and see a boy in there with the Triceratops and talking to him, and maybe even riding on his back, you can be pretty sure that boy will be me.